Obsessive Behavior Saga:

Renaissance Collection

Obsessive Behavior Saga:
Renaissance Collection

Dorothy Brown-Newton

www.urbanbooks.net

Urban Books, LLC
300 Farmingdale Road, NY-Route 109
Farmingdale, NY 11735

Obsessive Behavior Saga: Renaissance Collection

ISBN 13: 978-1-62286-552-9
ISBN 10: 1-62286-552-9

First Trade Paperback Printing February 2017
Printed in the United States of America

10 9 8 7 6 5 4 3 2 1

This is a work of fiction. Any references or similarities to actual events, real people, living or dead, or to real locales are intended to give the novel a sense of reality. Any similarity in other names, characters, places, and incidents is entirely coincidental.

Distributed by Kensington Publishing Corp.
Submit Orders to:
Customer Service
400 Hahn Road
Westminster, MD 21157-4627
Phone: 1-800-733-3000
Fax: 1-800-659-2436

KINDRAH

Amari called me and said he just wanted to hear my voice, being that he hadn't spoken to me all day. I wished I could tell him how I felt about him, but I knew I would be going against everything I believed in. I felt that no woman should pursue a man who was already involved with someone else. Amari and I shared a special friendship. We hung out together, we called each other all the time, and we gave each other advice pertaining to the relationships that we were in. I fell in love with him without even trying, if that makes any sense. I knew he had feelings for me as well, but I didn't know if he felt the same way I felt.

Anyway, let me stop daydreaming and get back to work, I thought. I hadn't done anything since his call.

I left work at 6 p.m. and went to the gym for about an hour. As soon as I made it home, I called Amari to see what he had planned for the evening. He said he and his father were going to catch a movie and asked if I wanted to join them. I didn't have any plans, so I accepted.

After I got out of the shower and before getting dressed, I called Raj to let him know I would be going out with Amari and his dad. He didn't sound too pleased, but what he failed to realize was that he was always working. I really hated coming home to an empty house. We didn't live together, but it would feel good to have him spend the night with me at least twice a week. Shit, we barely saw each other because I worked days and he worked evenings. I knew he felt some kind of way about my friendship with Amari, but he never stressed me because he knew Amari and I were friends when I met him.

One day I was picking Amari up from work because his car was at the shop, and I saw this fine chocolate brotha in front of his building. When I say fine, I mean fine as shit. He was six foot one with a dark brown complexion and light brown eyes. I knew I was looking cute in my Juicy Couture shorts that hugged my hips just right, so I stepped out of the car even though I didn't have a reason to. Once he saw me, it was a wrap. We exchanged numbers, and we'd been together for two years now. He never voiced his dislike of my friendship with Amari, but even if he did, I wouldn't stop being friends with Amari. We had a pact that no matter who we got involved with, we would not let them come between our friendship.

Now, Amari's girlfriend, Tanisha, had a very big problem with our relationship. She did all types of petty bullshit with her insecure ass. I told him to leave that childish little girl alone and find him a real woman. What I really wanted to tell him was he should find someone like his best friend—me.

AMARI

Kindrah parked her car in the garage and came in because we had to wait on my dad, who was driving us to the theatre. I heard a car and thought my dad was pulling up outside, but when I opened the door, I saw it was Tanisha.

Here we go. I was praying I didn't have to get into an argument with this girl.

"Hey, babe." She greeted me and gave me a kiss. We were good until she saw Kindrah come out of the house.

"Why the fuck is she here?" she asked, clearly irritated.

"Tanisha, please don't start. I told you I was going to the movies with my dad tonight," I said, hoping she would just go in the house.

"Yes, you did, but you failed to mention that Kindrah would be going."

Kindrah just shook her head. She knew Tanisha was about to show her ass, but she didn't say anything because we went through this all the time.

It was not just Tanisha; it was like no one could accept or believe that we were just friends because of how close we were.

"Look, Tanisha, you can either come with us or go in the house with all that bullshit. And why the fuck is your ass home early anyway?"

"First off, don't worry about why the fuck I'm home early. And if you wanted me to go, you would have invited me, so don't stand here and fucking act as if you want me to go. Every time I turn around, you're in this bitch's face and using your fucking father so that I think it's nothing, but I'm getting sick of this bullshit."

Kindrah gave me a look that said, *Get her before I do*.

"Tanisha, take your ass in the house. Believe what the fuck you want to believe," I said, letting her know that the conversation was over.

She ran up the steps and slammed the door. My dad was just pulling into the driveway. How fucking convenient. If his ass would have been there twenty minutes earlier, I wouldn't have had to deal with that crazy broad. I loved her, but she was fucking tripping all the time. I was pissed off and embarrassed at the same time. She always showed out in front of our neighbors.

EDWARD

Here I was, bearing witness to my son's attitude because of him and Tanisha arguing about Kindrah once again. I kind of felt sorry for Tanisha because I could really understand how she felt about my son and his "best friend." Anyone with eyes could see that they had something going on. The way Kindrah looked at him and the way she laid her head on his shoulder through the entire movie had me convinced, but my son insisted on telling me that they were just friends. Was I convinced? Hell no, and his ass should have been more careful. If he was telling the truth, he didn't know that Kindrah was in love with him. I had to have a man to man with my son to see what was really going on. If he and Kindrah were in fact more than friends, I didn't want him involving me. I liked Tanisha, and I didn't want her to think that I was out here helping my son have a relationship with Kindrah when they were claiming to only be friends.

KINDRAH

When I got home from the movies, Raj was in the living room watching ESPN. I could tell he had been drinking. I walked into the bedroom and started undressing. He walked in the room, stared at me for about a second, then grabbed me from behind and started kissing my neck. He was asking me if I had a good time while continuing to kiss me. I really wasn't in the mood. Anytime I went out with Amari, I liked to come home and think about him. Just the thought of him gave me a tingling sensation between my legs.

Raj must have thought I was responding to him because he finished undressing me. He began caressing my now erect nipples as he sucked on them nice and slow. As he laid me down on the bed, he began to slowly make his way down my body, kissing every inch until he reached between my legs. Don't get me wrong, Raj had it going on when it came to making love, but my mind was on the real love of my life.

I closed my eyes and made love to Amari. I know it was wrong to sleep with Raj while thinking of another man, but my love for Raj was physical, while Amari had my mind, body, and soul. It killed me knowing he belonged to someone else.

Don't look at it as me stringing Raj along, because I was not. In the beginning of our relationship, he was involved with someone, but he lied to me and told me that he wasn't. He only broke up with the female after we made it official. By the time I found out the truth, it was too late; I was already feeling him. But now, between his work schedule and spending time with his daughter, he hadn't really been giving me the attention that I craved—not to mention the fact that I always caught him lying about everything.

Raj was asleep, something he always did right after sex. There was no, "Do you want something to drink?" or,

"Do you need a washcloth?" There damn sure was no cuddling. Just straight to sleep. I had gotten up to go in the bathroom to shower when my phone chirped, telling me I had a text message. I smiled at his name on the screen. It read:

Hey. Just wanted to say thanks for hanging out with me and my old man. LOL. And I apologize for Tanisha being disrespectful, and I appreciate how you handled it. I know you said nothing on the strength of me. She was really out of line, and the situation could have gotten out of hand. Again, thanks for being you.

I closed the phone without responding because my feelings were now all over the place. Oh, how I loved me some him.

TANISHA

This Negro had some fucking nerve walking in here smelling like that bitch's perfume. Amari must have really thought I was fucking stupid. If nothing was going on, why did he fail to mention that Kindrah was going when he told me he and his dad were going to the movies? He didn't expect me to get home early. He figured he would have left before I got home from work, but I had to leave early because I wasn't feeling well. It only made matters worse that I had to come home to see this bitch looking at me with that smirk on her face. You damn right I went off, and I was hoping that bitch popped off; but she didn't because she knew Amari was going to come to her defense like he always did. I fell back when I saw the look that Amari was giving me for calling his precious Kindrah a bitch.

I thought twice about continuing the name calling when I realized I was playing myself in front of the neighbors once again, so I just went inside and slammed the door. But to see Amari not even consider my feelings and still leave with that bitch, my feeling were hurt again. I didn't cry this time. I had no tears left.

Amari and Kindrah's friendship would be done sooner or later. I was going to break up this "friendship" one way or another. Mark my words—this shit was going to stop.

MEESHA

Karen called to ask if I wanted to go to the club. She was starting to get on my nerves. Every weekend she called, asking me to go out. I knew she was only doing what best friends do, but after losing the love of my life, I really didn't have the strength to go out and start meeting men, let alone date anyone.

"Listen here, chica. I will be at your house at exactly eleven p.m., and you better be ready to go. I'm tired of you going to work and then coming home sulking. Trey is gone. I understand how you're feeling, but Me-Me, it's been almost eight months. Come on, baby girl, it's time for you to get out of this funk. I'm not saying go out and fuck the first man you see. I'm not even saying go out and meet anyone. Just come out and hang with the girls. We miss you."

I held the phone in my hand, all teary-eyed, but I agreed to go out.

I showered and decided that I wasn't going to get all dressed up. The less attention I received, the better. I wore some black spandex with an open-back red halter top. I slid into my four-inch heels that I had picked up from Baker's the day before. Once Karen, Stephanie, and Tisha got to my house, we were ready to go.

All eyes were on us as we walked into the club. We all looked good, and Stephanie's homeboy, Kevin, got us VIP status, so that was a plus. The waitress came by with a bottle of Coconut Cîroc and some Absolut, compliments of Kevin. I wasn't much of a drinker, so I sipped on my drink, thinking about my baby Trey. I missed him so much. Steph and Trina were on the dance floor, doing what they did best, looking for their next sleeping partners.

As I looked across the room, I noticed a group of guys from my job. I recognized Raj, Vince, Amari, and a couple of other familiar faces. It must have been some type of birthday party for one of the guys because I never saw Raj and Amari really hang like that. I knew Amari and Raj's girl, Kindrah, were cool, but that's about it. Raj always made small talk whenever I would see him at work, but I was always in a somber mood, so I really didn't give anyone the time of day. I just did my job and went home.

The guys were now posted up two tables down from where I was sitting. Raj noticed me and walked over, starting to make small talk again. He seemed nervous. I smiled to myself, thinking, *How cute*. I didn't know if it was because I was sipping, but he was actually handsome. I never really noticed before. He sat with me for the rest of the evening, and we talked about everything but work. I really enjoyed his company. I felt safe with him, knowing he had a girlfriend.

His cell went off, and when I heard him saying that he was still at the party and "Your boy Amari is here too," I knew he was speaking to his girl. I felt a pang of jealousy, but I choked it up real fast. He ended the call, told me he had to go, and that he would see me at work.

KINDRAH

Raj thought I had an attitude with him, but I didn't. I was upset once he told me that Amari was at the club. I'd been calling his ass all night, and he had yet to answer. When Raj went into the bathroom to shower, I texted Amari to call me ASAP. It took him all of five minutes to call back, and as soon as I said hello, he knew I was upset. He started apologizing, saying that he didn't hear the phone because of the music. I was just happy to hear his voice, so I didn't make a big deal about it. We talked for a few more minutes, and I told him I would speak with him later.

Raj came out of the bathroom, hopped into bed, and was out within minutes. I just stared up at the ceiling, thinking about the true love of my life. I was really tired of living this lie I called my life. No matter how hard I tried, this lonely and empty feeling was a constant reminder of what I wanted and what I was missing. I had tried talking to Raj on several occasions, telling him that I wanted and needed more in the relationship. He always promised to be more attentive and do better as far as us doing things together as a couple, but to no avail. So when he had an issue with me hanging out with Amari more than I hung with him, I didn't feel bad. How many times did I have to tell him that I didn't feel like we were together as boyfriend and girlfriend? It felt like more of a roommate arrangement when he did decide to stay over.

AMARI

When I got in, I saw that Kindrah had called several times, and then she texted me to give her a call. I spoke with her for a few, and when I hung up the phone, it seemed as if Tanisha had other plans. She pushed me back on the bed and started undressing me. She kissed my neck, then moved up to my lips and kissed me like she was never going to see me again. I returned her kiss and removed her nightgown, noticing she wasn't wearing any panties. As if on cue, my dick poked at my jeans, begging to be released; but this was Tanisha's show, so I let her do her thing.

She began teasing the head of my penis, licking in a circular motion and sucking the head like it was a lollipop. I closed my eyes as I felt her deep-throat my joint without gagging. I grabbed her head as I fucked her mouth until I came, and she swallowed every drop. I didn't know what had gotten into her, but I loved it.

It took me all of a minute before my shit was hard again and standing at attention. I lifted her up, and now her sexy shaved vagina was in my face. I dug in as if it was my last meal. She tasted so sweet and was bucking like crazy, so I knew she was on the verge of exploding. I sucked up all her juices, flipped her into the doggie-style position, and tore that ass up. I was about to cum again, so I changed positions. She was now riding my dick reverse style. I didn't know what had gotten into her, but I loved this shit. Tanisha was riding my shit like she was at the rodeo going for first prize. We came together and passed out together.

KINDRAH

It had been a stressful day at work. My supervisor had been getting on my nerves lately with petty bullshit, probably because she was not getting any dick at home. I wanted to tell her, "Don't come to work taking that shit out on me; I'm not the one! I do my work on time, so leave me the fuck alone." However, once I started thinking about what I had to look forward to that night, her pettiness didn't even matter. Tanisha was giving Amari a birthday party, and I couldn't wait to see him again.

I had been noticing a change in Raj. He seemed more distant than before, and he hadn't been calling or texting me as much as he used to. He also started dressing different and wearing cologne, which shocked the hell out of me. I'd bought him so many bottles over the years, and he had never touched one, talking about he didn't like wearing it, so I stopped buying them. He hadn't even been staying the night anymore, but it was all good. He only came over this night because I invited him to go with me to Amari's birthday party.

We arrived at the party a little after 10 p.m. Tanisha had gone all out. The place was a beautiful, intimate club located near the water. If you looked out of the bay windows, the light that illuminated the water gave it a romantic setting. The club was decorated with a gold-and-black theme. It was breathtaking, and the music was on point.

Amari was sitting at a table with a drink in his hand, talking to his dad, and Tanisha was sitting with him. I walked over, and he stood up to hug me, kissing me on the cheek. I wished him a happy birthday and said hello to Tanisha and his dad. Raj gave Amari dap, and I sat down while Raj left to go to the bar to get us drinks.

I really wasn't feeling watching this bitch sitting all up in Amari's lap and kissing on him, so I turned to the dance floor. While trying to avoid that scene, I noticed Raj at the bar, talking to some bitch. He was smiling and being a little too comfortable with this bitch.

When he came back to the table, I asked him who he was talking to at the bar, and he said it was his coworker, Meesha. I let it go with a roll of my eyes because I wasn't trying to get into it with him on Amari's night. We got on the dance floor and started getting our dance on. Amari came and cut in, so now he and I were dancing. I was getting turned on. He smelled so good. We danced to one last song and headed over to the table because Tanisha had an announcement to make. I saw Raj dancing with his coworker, Meesha, who he had been all smiles with minutes earlier. I gave him a look as if to say it was okay, but I was pissed.

The DJ made another announcement for everyone to take their seats. I took a seat, waiting to see what announcement this chick had to make. She was so extra.

"I just want to thank everyone for coming out and celebrating Amari's birthday with us." Everyone clapped. Tanisha proceeded to walk over to him, standing in front of him while holding his hands. She continued. "Amari, words can't explain how much you mean to me. We have had our ups and downs, but nothing, and I do mean nothing, will ever come between us. I love you, babe. Happy birthday."

I kind of felt that her speech was directed to me as she kissed him on the lips and handed him a gift bag. When he opened the bag and pulled out his gift, it made me feel light-headed, as if I was going to faint. It got so hot, and the room felt like it was spinning. I felt like I couldn't breathe. I heard all of the clapping and people saying congrats. I looked over just to be sure, and sure enough, he was holding up a pair of baby booties.

As he got up to hug and kiss her, he told her she had given him the best birthday present ever. I needed to get some air before I showed my true feelings. I told Raj that I was ready to go because I wasn't feeling well. I didn't know if he picked up on why I needed to leave, but I really didn't care as long as he got me out of there.

TANISHA

Revenge is sweet. The look on Kindrah's face when Amari opened the bag was priceless. I had gone to Babies R Us earlier that day and bought a pair of baby booties. When I handed him the bag and he pulled out the booties, he didn't get what I was trying to tell him, so I whispered in his ear and told him he was going to be a father. He picked me up, kissed me, and told me that he loved me. I felt so good inside.

I looked over in the direction that Kindrah had been in, but she was no longer there. I was trying to figure out why she would leave. Her and Amari claimed to only be friends, and what friend leaves a friend's party without saying congrats or good night? I knew there was more to that friendship bullshit than what they were trying to sell.

Oh well, bitch. It's time you find another friend because once me and Amari are married, your ass will be history. Believe that, I thought.

The rest of the night went okay, but my happy mood didn't last too long. Once Amari saw that Kindrah had left, it was like his whole mood had changed, and it was pissing me off. I was so ready to go before I showed out in front of friends and family.

AMARI

Kindrah didn't even say good-bye, congrats, or anything. I wondered if she and Raj had gotten into it, because that wasn't like her at all. I hoped she hadn't seen him doing anything stupid being that Meesha was at the party. Lately he had been seen with her a lot, and I was wondering if I should have said something to her about it. It looked like Raj was creeping.

I texted her, but she didn't respond. I knew Raj wouldn't be at the crib because this was his weekend to have his daughter, so I was sure he had to go and pick her up from his mom. I decided that once the party was over and I dropped Tanisha off, I would go by and check on her.

Now, although I was happy about being a father, I was curious as to how. Tanisha and I had decided that we were going to wait until we were married to have children, and she was supposed to be on the pill. I guess we would discuss that later.

After the party was over, I walked my dad to his car, and he told me to come by the house the next time I had a day off. Tanisha was upset when I dropped her off because I told her that I would be back, but I wasn't really concerned with her attitude. I had to go make sure Kindrah was okay, and I would just have to deal with the argument later. I would not be able to sleep knowing something was bothering Kindrah and I didn't check on her.

KINDRAH

My phone rang, and I answered it with an attitude. I really didn't feel like being bothered by anyone, but to my surprise, it was Amari telling me to open the door. Once he was in, I couldn't help but smile at the thought of Tanisha having a fit because he had left the house. No doubt, she knew he was coming here to check on me. I sat on the couch, and he sat on the other side of the room, looking pissed off.

"Yo, tell me something. How do you claim to be my best friend and have love for a nigga, but you leave my party without saying congrats or good-bye? That's some fucked up shit, and it really hurts because I really didn't expect that from you."

I just looked at him because he looked upset, and I didn't know how to answer the question. I must have taken too long to answer him because he went over to the bar to fix a drink, slamming shit around. He came back and sat down and looked at me, waiting for me to answer his question. I looked him in his eyes as I felt the tears trying to fall. I took a deep breath and decided to just be honest with him, because this conversation was long overdue.

"Okay, Amari, I'm going to be honest with you. The reason I left your party without saying anything is because I couldn't stay and pretend like I was happy that you are about to become a father. I have loved you for as long as I have known you, and I'm not talking about the kind of love friends have between each other. I have been in love with you from the day you came into my life." The tears I had tried to hold back were now streaming down my face.

"I know I should have probably said something a long time ago, but you had Tanisha, so I was just happy being your friend," I continued. "But when the reality of it hit me tonight, that you're going to be a father and possibly someone's husband, I had to get out of there. I do apologize."

He got up off of the couch and started pacing back and forth. He wouldn't even look at me. He set his glass down on the bar and walked out the door with no words said.

I couldn't move. I was so hurt, and the tears wouldn't stop. I knew I had to pull myself together as I got up, walked over to the door, locked it, and went to my bedroom. I put in my Tamia CD and played the third track. I listened to "Almost" on repeat until I fell asleep.

AMARI

I couldn't believe Kindrah said she loved me. I didn't know what to say, and I didn't know how to feel, so I just walked out. How could she just go and flip the script on me? What part of the game was that? I had love for her, but I never looked at her that way. She was my best friend. I just hoped we could continue to be friends, but somehow I knew that the friendship would never be the same.

A couple of weeks went by, and I had yet to speak to Kindrah. She didn't try to call me, and I didn't call her. I was going crazy without her in my life. I really needed my friend right now, but I didn't know how to feel. I wanted to call her, but I didn't know what to say. I was hoping that she called me first so that I wouldn't have to, but she never did.

I decided to go visit my dad. He'd been asking me to stop by. Truth be told, I had been avoiding everyone. I'd been going to work, gym, and then home.

My dad was happy to see me, but right away he could tell that something was bothering me. He and Kindrah were the only ones who knew me like that. My dad and my mom separated when I was eight years old, but he had always been a part of my life. My mom passed away a year ago, and without him and Kindrah, I didn't know how I would have continued living. I was so thankful for the two of them.

My father saw the look on my face, and he came and sat next to me. "Look, son," he said. "You know I don't get involved in your personal business unless it's necessary. I know you told me that you and Kindrah are only friends, and I want to believe you, but let me tell you, for anyone on the outside looking in, it looks as though you two are messing around. I raised you to be a man, and you're about to be a father. You have to do what's right for Tanisha and your child."

I guess I was the only one that hadn't picked up on it, because I had no idea that Kindrah had feelings for me like that, and I didn't think that we were acting like a couple at all.

"Dad, when I say that Kindrah and I are only friends, that's the truth. The night of my party, I noticed that Kindrah left the party without saying anything. When I dropped Tanisha off, I went by her house to see if she was all right because I thought her and Raj got into a fight. Once I got there, she told me she left the party because she was hurt that I was about to be a father. I was confused, because if anyone was going to be happy for me, I knew it would be her, my best friend. She saw that I was upset, so she told me that she loved me from the first time she met me. I was taken aback because I never knew she felt that way. She never gave off that she had those feelings for me."

"Son, I see the love in her eyes when she looks at you. Even Tanisha knows that Kindrah loves you. You're the only one walking around with blinders on," he said.

"Son, when I married your mother, I did it because she got pregnant and I felt that was the right thing to do. But you see, marriage doesn't work when you don't marry for love. Now, don't get me wrong. I loved your mother, but I wasn't in love, nor was I content or happy, which led to divorce," he explained.

"I don't want you to make the same mistakes I've made. I know you love Tanisha, but I also know that you aren't ready to have children without marriage. It's a new day, son. You can be there for your child without being married. I'm not saying you have to walk away, either, unless that's what you feel you want to do.

"I don't know if you have feelings for Kindrah, but when I see you two together, you look happy. I don't see that same love in your eyes when you're with Tanisha, so with that being said, I will support you with whatever decision you make. I love you, son."

"I love you too, Dad."

I chilled with my dad for a little while before I headed out. I felt much better after talking to my dad, and I needed to talk to Kindrah to figure this thing out, because I missed my friend.

KINDRAH

I had just got off the phone with Raj, and we decided to go our separate ways. It was not like I was upset. I hadn't seen him in a month. I mean, we talked on the phone, but whenever I asked if he was coming over, he would tell me that he had his daughter. I really just needed someone there to try to fill a void. I missed Amari so much. Work had been an outlet, but after six o'clock I just went home and dwelled in my loneliness. I even stopped going to the gym. I had been so depressed that I felt like packing my things, leaving everything behind, and starting over. It was not like I had family there or any real friends who would miss me.

I heard that Tanisha was pregnant with twins, and that was when I really lost it. I didn't even know that I had any tears left. That was supposed to be me laying with him every night and having his babies. Why hadn't I told him how I felt years ago?

I couldn't stop the tears from falling from my eyes. I was so hurt, but I couldn't just sit and do nothing. I grabbed my keys off of the table. I had to go see him. How could he not reach out to me? Didn't he know I was hurting right now? Why wouldn't he reach out to me?

The hurt was being replaced with anger, because he knew I had no one right now. I rushed out to my car as I tried not to get wet from the downpour. The tears started again. I almost went back inside because I hated driving in the rain. As I pulled out of the driveway, I was crying hard and not paying attention to the truck swaying my way until it was too late. I felt a sharp pain on the side of my head, then darkness.

AMARI

After talking to my father, I finally decided to go talk to Kindrah. When I pulled up to her block, I saw the ambulance, police, and neighbors standing outside. I was scared to move. I saw Kindrah's car turned over, and my heart broke into a million pieces. I had to get to her. I jumped out of my car and ran over but was stopped by the police officers. I looked up and saw them working on her in the ambulance.

Please, Kindrah, don't let this be your end. I didn't get the chance to tell you how I really feel about you.

The last thing I remembered was confessing my love to her and trying to make it to the ambulance. Unfortunately, it was too late. As I saw them pull off, I fell to my knees.

TANISHA

Yeah, bitch, I knew he was on his way to you. Why couldn't you just leave us alone? I knew I couldn't compete with the type of relationship that you two had, but I was willing to do whatever was needed to make him see how much I really loved him. I even sacrificed my body to give him a child when I don't even like children. Why did you have to go and confess your love for him? Now look at what you made me do! I never wanted to hurt you, but you just wouldn't back off and leave well enough alone. So die, bitch. I will be here helping my man cope with your death.

I had sat back these last couple of weeks watching Amari in his depressed state because he and Kindrah weren't speaking. His cousin told me that Kindrah told him that she loved him and they had a falling out. I was just happy that he wasn't calling her or going to see her.

When I saw that his mood was a little better, I knew that something had changed. He had either spoken to her or he was going to see her. When I checked his phone, I didn't see any communication between them, so I knew his ass was going to see her.

AMARI

I was in the middle of the street, down on my knees. I was praying that my eyes were deceiving me. I couldn't believe I wouldn't get the chance to tell Kindrah how I felt about her. My heart hurt so bad that it was hard to breathe. I didn't even care that I was in the middle of the street, getting soaked from the rain, because my tears blended in with the downpour.

I felt someone touch me lightly on my shoulder. I looked up to see two female police officers.

"Sir, are you Amari James?"

My vision was slightly blurred. I wiped at my eyes and managed to say yes.

"Come with me, sir. I'm Officer Jenkins, and this is my partner, Officer Creer. We just got a call on the radio saying EMS were able to revive Ms. Kindrah Watts, and she's asking for you. We need to hurry and get you to the hospital."

I couldn't believe what I was hearing. The officers saw that I was in shock upon hearing that Kindrah was still alive. I continued to stand in the same spot, unable to move, until they assisted me toward the patrol car, helping me in.

TANISHA

I sat in my truck in a panic as I watched the police officers escort Amari to the waiting police car. Did they suspect that he was the one who caused the accident and Kindrah's untimely death? My mind was throwing all types of scenarios of why Amari was being arrested.

I couldn't stop my hands from shaking as I started banging my head on the steering wheel and shouted, "This isn't happening the way I planned! Amari was supposed to get the news that Kindrah was in a car accident and didn't make it due to her injuries."

He was to come home distraught, and I would be there to help him grieve his so-called best friend. With Kindrah gone, Amari and I could get married, raise our twins, and live happily ever after, or so I thought. Now my man was being arrested for a crime I had committed.

I waited until the scene died down and all of the police cars left before pulling out of the spot that I was in at the end of the block. I had to find somewhere to park the truck until I could get the damages fixed.

I left the truck two blocks away from the auto shop that I was going to use to fix the damages to the vehicle. I called a car service to take me home to wait on Amari's phone call. I needed to know if he needed me to come down to the police station.

AMARI

I was nervous walking into the hospital. The smell of the building and its dingy walls always made me think of death, and today was no different. My legs felt as if they would give out at any minute. The officers stopped at the front desk to speak with the nurse in the emergency department. When the officers turned to speak with me, I knew something wasn't right, due to the look of sympathy on their faces.

Officer Creer put her hand on my shoulder. She let me know that Kindrah was put in a medically induced coma due to swelling on the brain, and that a doctor would come out and speak with me. The officers said that they would keep me in their prayers and handed me their cards. They said that they would be in touch while the investigation was being done. Right now, this was being considered a hit and run accident. I thanked them before walking off to sit in the room to wait for the doctor.

KINDRAH

I felt myself in a deep sleep, like I was caught in a dream. I remembered being in a car accident and losing consciousness, but now I could hear voices all around me. I heard someone shouting "Clear!" and then I felt my body rise and fall as my eyes fluttered and opened. I also remembered someone asking me if I knew what had happened to me, but I only asked for Amari. I heard someone ask me to repeat myself, and that's when I got frustrated and yelled, "Amari James!"

Next, I felt my body start to convulse, and then I was drifting back off into darkness. I could hear the sounds of alarms beeping, but not much of anything else. I remembered how I was feeling just before I decided to go visit Amari.

I was hurt, depressed, and refusing to eat. I couldn't understand how Amari could just walk away from me because I had told him my true feelings. Yes, I was in love with him and had been for years. Yes, I had been in a couple of relationships, but I still felt empty inside because Amari was the love of my life. I felt that even if he wasn't in love with me, he didn't have to walk out of my life the way he had. I knew he loved me as a friend, so that should have been enough to stick around and talk about what I had just confessed.

Truth be told, he was all I had. I was the only survivor of the fire that claimed my parents' and siblings' lives. I had been at a friend's birthday sleepover party when the fire swept through our home. No family members came forward to claim me, so I was put in foster care. That was how I met Amari. His family lived on the same block as my foster parents. Amari was my lifeline. He was there when I needed an outlet from my abusive foster parents.

Both of my foster parents were alcoholics, so how they were able to be foster parents was a mystery to me. Their home was never well kept, and they rarely went food shopping, but with the backlog at the Children's Services Department, the worker rarely made visits.

AMARI

The doctor entered the waiting room, introducing himself as Dr. Kaufman. He explained that the head injury Kindrah suffered from the accident caused her brain to swell and bleed, pushing the fluid against her skull. He said that the swelling could eventually cause the brain to push down on the brain stem, which can damage the reticular activating system. He saw that I was looking at him like I was confused, so he explained that it was the part of the brain that's responsible for arousal and awareness. He also explained that Kindrah was put in a medically induced coma until some of the swelling went down.

"Doctor, will she have a full recovery?" I asked.

"Right now, we are hoping that the swelling goes down on its own. Surgery may also be necessary to relieve the pressure on the brain due to the swelling. We are monitoring her, but it's too early to tell right now if she will have a full recovery. The next forty-eight hours will give us a better understanding of what methods to employ. I assure you, Mr. James, we are the best at what we do, and we will do all that we can to care for Ms. Watts. Also, I want to prepare you for when you go to her room to visit. Her face has a lot a swelling. She is alive and looks as if she is sleeping, but in this coma she will not be awakened by any stimulation, including pain."

I was in deep thought after listening to what the doctor told me. I called my father because I was going to need all the support I could get, and truth be told, my family was the only family she had.

I was nervous and my body felt warm all over as I walked down the hallway to the ICU. When I walked into the room and saw her, I broke down. Kindrah had a cast on her right arm, and her face was black and blue, swollen to where she was almost unrecognizable.

I sat beside her bed and held her hand, telling her how sorry I was that I had walked out of her life. I had been scared that if I told her that I felt the same way, knowing that we had significant others, things would have been difficult. I didn't want to lose the friendship, which didn't make sense, because I still ended up leaving the friendship when I walked out of her house.

Kindrah's accident was really taking a toll on my body. I had been sleeping at the hospital for the past two weeks, only leaving to shower and change clothes. Every day I made sure not to be gone too long because I wanted to be the first person she saw when she woke up. The doctors reported some improvements in her condition. Most of the swelling had gone down, and she was identifiable again.

Tanisha wasn't dealing too well with me being at the hospital and not at home with her, since she was pregnant with my babies. Even though I agreed that she had every right to feel the way she did, I told her a million times that I was the only family Kindrah had. Raj visited once or twice, but with him being in a new relationship and working, his time was limited. I took a personal leave from work, which didn't sit well with Tanisha either.

Detective Creer stopped by the hospital, letting me know that Kindrah's accident wasn't an accident. They said that they had a witness to the accident, and the details were still being investigated. She promised that she would keep in touch as the investigation progressed. I couldn't understand who would try to hurt Kindrah intentionally. Anyone who knew her liked her. She didn't have many friends, but she did go out once in a while with a couple of her coworkers. She had no enemies to my knowledge.

I sat drowning in my thoughts, trying to figure out if Kindrah had mentioned anybody she might have had a problem with. I was interrupted by the nurse on duty.

TANISHA

I just can't understand what went wrong. I saw them put that damn sheet over her head. Why is this bitch still breathing?

I was in total shock when I found out that Amari wasn't being arrested but was being rushed to the hospital because this bitch was asking for my man on her death bed. I should have just slit her fucking throat and made sure she stopped breathing. Amari's ass had been up at that hospital since this shit happened, and then he called to tell me that it wasn't an accident. They had a witness who said he had information about that night. Who the hell was out that time of night with the rain and darkness? I swear I saw no one.

I really didn't know how much more of this I could take before I snapped. I was pregnant with his fucking twins, and still he insisted on being at that bitch's side. Now I had to go and suck off this fat, ugly, stinky motherfucking detective to find out the information I needed. Once I got what I needed, he would never have the satisfaction of getting his dick sucked again, unless they had fucking and sucking in hell.

Once I got the information, I made sure that the detective was taken care of as he slept. I wiped down everything in the hotel room and removed all of my belongings, making sure to cover my tracks. The room was in his name, so I had no worries.

I took the information that I got from the detective and put it to use. I had been following Kindrah's neighbor for a few days, and he had the same routine daily. I decided that night would be the night, and now there I was, sitting outside of the Sugar Shack, waiting for him to leave the dirty little hole in the wall they called a strip joint.

After waiting nearly two hours, I finally saw him walk out. As he staggered his way to his car, I pulled up and followed behind him, calling out to him, asking him if he wanted to have a good time. He looked behind him, not believing that I was talking to him. He pointed to himself, and I nodded yes. He walked over to the car and got in. His eyes showed a look of surprise, seeing my baby bump, but it didn't bother him as much once he looked up and saw my double Ds threatening to fall out of my blouse.

I drove a few blocks over to a dark alley near a couple of abandoned buildings. I wanted to make this as quick as possible, so I let his seat all the way back and positioned myself onto his lap as best I could with his belly and all. He lifted my shirt and started to caress my breasts, and I tried not to vomit from the smell that was emanating from his body.

He was so into what he was doing, but he never got the chance to enjoy what he thought was going to be the best night of his life. In one quick motion, I sliced his throat. I opened the passenger's side door and pushed him out of the car, gasping and fighting for his last breath.

AMARI

The nurse came in the room to take Kindrah's vitals. She made small talk until she was done. Once she left, I pulled my chair close to her bed, held her hand, and spoke from my heart. My father told me that if I spoke to her, she would hear me even though she couldn't respond. I didn't know how true it was, but I sure as hell was going to try.

"Kindrah, if you can hear me, I just want you to know that I love you and I miss you. I'm so sorry that I walked away when you told me how you felt. These past few weeks I have been dying not having you in my life, and that's when I realized nothing else mattered. I need you just as much as you need me, and I swear I was on my way to your house to tell you that I felt the same way. Please, wake up. I know what I did was wrong, and I'm sorry."

I didn't realize I was crying until I saw my tears hitting Kindrah's hand. As I went to wipe at my eyes, I felt the bed move. Kindrah's body shifted, and she was trying to move her legs. I jumped up and screamed for help. The nurse assigned to Kindrah rushed in, and so did the doctor.

I stood off to the side as I watched Kindrah's eyes flutter for a few seconds and then open. She looked scared. Dr. Kaufman started asking Kindrah all kinds of questions. He asked her to follow his finger as he moved it from right to left. He proceeded to ask her if she remembered what had happened to her, and if she knew where she was. She was able to follow his finger, and she knew she was in the hospital, but she didn't remember the accident. After about twenty minutes, the doctor gave the nurse orders for Kindrah's medication and blood work to be done.

I pulled my chair back over to the bed as soon as they left the room.

"Hey, how are you feeling? Do you need me to get you anything?" I asked, not knowing what else to say.

"No, I'm fine. What happened to me, and how long was I in a coma?" she asked, her voice not sounding like her own.

I bit down on my bottom lip, a habit I had when I wasn't sure how to explain something. I decided to give it to her straight, no chaser. Once I was done telling her, she gasped.

"Were you here the whole time? Because you look like you're really in need of some rest." She smiled.

It felt good seeing her smile. I missed her so much. I took her hands and started to speak again from the heart, this time knowing she was going to hear me. That alone had me nervous.

"Look, Kindrah, I just want to say I'm sorry for walking away from you and not telling you how I really feel about you. The truth is, you were with Raj and I'm with Tanisha, and she's pregnant. I didn't want to hurt her or get in between what you and Raj had going on. You're my best friend, and I always loved you. I just didn't want to ruin the friendship we have. I know I handled the situation the wrong way, and for that, I'm sorry."

"So what now?" she asked.

"If you give me some time to make things right, I would love for us to take a chance with a relationship, as long as we both promise to always be friends if it doesn't work out."

When she nodded her head to say okay, I leaned in and kissed her softly on her lips. I sat in deep thought as I watched Kindrah drift off to sleep from the medication. How was I going to tell Tanisha, my girlfriend of three years, that it was over and I wanted to be with my best friend? The best friend that I claimed so many times was only my friend.

It was the day Kindrah was finally being released from the hospital with strict instructions. She was to have physical therapy twice a week until she was able to gain strength in her right arm. Fortunately, Kindrah was expected to make a full recovery.

My father and I arrived at the hospital to take her home. Once Kindrah was settled in, I kissed her and told her that once I took care of what we spoke about, I would be hers. She smiled, but it wasn't a convincing smile. It was one of those smiles that let me know that she didn't believe me.

KINDRAH

It had been two months since my accident, and Amari had yet to leave Tanisha. I had finally gone back to work, and one day was a particularly stressful day. I really needed a drink, so when my coworker, Antwan, asked me if he could take me out for dinner, I said yes. I wasn't in the mood to be sitting home, not doing anything, on another Friday night by myself.

After I got out of the shower, I went to my closet to find something to wear. I decided on a pair of black Seven jeans with my V-neck, multi-print sweater, and a pair of black pumps. I looked at myself in the mirror and was pleased with my casual attire for my causal outing with a friend. It took me all of thirty minutes to be ready and out the door to meet Antwan at the restaurant. I decided I wasn't ready for him to know where I lived just yet.

Antwan was already waiting at the bar when I got there. He was looking good in his black True Religion jeans, a burgundy button-up, and a pair of burgundy Prada sneakers. He was wearing D&G's Light Blue cologne. I was very familiar with the scent, and it was still intoxicating.

Once we were seated, I started to get nervous. I hadn't been out in so long with anyone.

"So, Ms. Kindrah, tell me something about yourself that I don't already know."

"Well, you know where I work. I'm single, and I don't have any kids. I love a quiet night at home, on my couch, watching old movies. I love to read, and I also dabble with the pen once in a while, writing poetry. I have no family. I have a best friend, but mostly it's just me, myself, and I."

"Well, we have some things in common. My mother passed away last year from breast cancer. I never knew my father. I'm an only child, and I also like to watch old movies. Maybe next time we could have a movie night."

"Ha, what makes you think it will be a next time?" I asked, smiling.

Just as he was about to answer, the waitress came to take our order. I ordered the ribs with fries and coleslaw, and Antwan ordered the baked chicken with shrimp scampi. Once the order was taken, he got right back to it.

"Okay, back to the matter at hand. Ms. Kindrah, it would be my pleasure to have a second date with you. And before you answer, ask yourself how you could resist having a second date with me." He smiled, and his dimples made me smile. He was handsome, and I was really enjoying my time with him.

We continued talking until our food came. When dinner was over, I was a little sad to see my dinner date come to an end. Antwan paid the check and left a nice tip. He walked me to my car and kissed me on the cheek. He told me he had a good time and that he looked forward to doing it again.

"Call me to let me know you made it home, sexy," he said as I got in my car.

When I pulled off, I had a permanent smile on my face. I hadn't felt this good in a long time, and I was glad I had agreed to go out.

When I pulled up to my house, I saw Amari's car, but he wasn't in it. Before I got a chance to put my key in the door, he opened it, looking at me like I had two heads.

"I've been sitting here for hours waiting for you. Where were you?" he asked.

"Excuse me? I didn't know I needed to clock in, and why didn't you just call me like you always do?"

"I would have called, but I figured you were working late. By looking at your outfit, I see that's not the case. So again, where are you coming from?"

"I went out to dinner with a friend from work, if you must know," I answered.

He turned around like he hadn't heard me correctly. "You went where with who?"

"I went out to dinner with a friend from work. I didn't stutter."

"So you went out with some dude when we're supposed to be trying to be together?"

"Amari, miss me with the bullshit. It's been two fucking months, and you still have yet to leave Tanisha. That's fine. She's about to be the mother of your children, and she needs you. I was being selfish by putting my needs and wants before your soon-to-be children, and I don't feel right doing that. As much as I love you, I think it would be best that we just remain friends," I told him.

If looks could kill, I would have been dead. He stared at me for a few seconds then walked over to me and kissed me.

"Amari, don't do this," I said, trying to ignore the feeling I was now having between my legs.

He moved from my lips and started kissing me on my neck. I was no longer in control of my body, so I stopped fighting it. I'd been waiting for this for so long.

He led me to my bedroom and started to undress me while proceeding to undress himself. I felt like this was my first time. It was kind of foreign to me. This man, who I had loved all my life as my friend, was about to give me the one thing I wanted for forever, and I was nervous like a virgin who was about to have sex for the first time.

I asked him if he could put on the radio because I needed something soothing to get my nerves in check. The Quiet Storm was on, and I relaxed a little. We started kissing, and my body felt warm all over. I felt like I was having an out of body experience.

I became the aggressor, pushing him on his back and kissing him. I climbed on top of him and continued kissing him. The kiss felt magical.

He released my lips, and we changed positions with me now lying on my back. Amari began to kiss the inside of my thighs. My vagina was giving me a tingling sensation as I waited for his tongue to touch my prized possession. When his lips hit that spot and his tongue kissed my opening, my juices started flowing. If this was what heaven felt like, I didn't mind dying that night.

I guess Amari couldn't take it anymore. He flipped me over in the doggy-style position and fucked me into a coma. I couldn't move. I was exhausted and satisfied, but Amari wasn't done yet. He told me to stand. Was he serious? Then he said to bend over and touch my toes.

I stood up on wobbly legs and did what he asked. I touched my toes because I was curious, but when I felt his nine and a half inches inside me again, I moaned. He began to hit my spot nice and slow at first, and then he went in for the kill. I tried to keep my balance and throw the pussy at him as best as I could. I would have told him to stop, but it hurt so good.

Amari picked up his pace, going even faster, and I knew he was about to cum. He made a sound that scared me a little while grabbing my hair. As he came, I came with him. He was never this good in my dreams. If I knew he had it going on like this, I would have told him my true feelings years ago.

We showered together, then I cuddled with him, listening to his breathing as he drifted off to sleep.

My cell phone alerted me that I had a text message. I reached over Amari and grabbed my phone. It was a text from Antwan.

Hey, Ms. Kindrah. You didn't call me to let me know you made it home safely. I hope all is well. And I just wanted to say thanks for having dinner with me, and I look forward to seeing you again. Hit me back to let me know that you're okay.

I felt bad. I had forgotten to text him when I came in, so I sent him a quick response.

Hey, Antwan. I do apologize. When I got home, I hopped in the shower. I started watching one of my old movies and dozed off. And I really enjoyed your company tonight as well. Thanks for checking on me. I'll see you at work on Monday, and we can discuss a second outing, Mr. Dimples. Goodnight.

I put the phone back on the nightstand and laid my head on Amari's chest. He wrapped his arm around me, and I soon drifted off into a peaceful sleep.

TANISHA

Amari hadn't come home the night before, and I swear to God, if my feet weren't swollen and that doctor hadn't put me on bed rest, I would have been out there looking for his ass. I called him numerous times, and his ass had the nerve to not pick up the phone. What if it had been an emergency? I was almost six months pregnant, and he knew that the doctor said that I needed to take it easy, so why the hell wouldn't he bring his ass home from work? No call or nothing, and his damn father had the nerve to say that he didn't know where he was and that he hadn't spoken to him all day. Did I believe him? No, I didn't, but what I did know was that Amari had better get his shit right before I forgot that I loved his ass.

I started to call Kindrah's ass but decided against it. My home girl had told me she saw Kindrah out with some dude the night before, so where the fuck was Amari?

I tried calling his phone again but still got his voice mail. I decided to go to bed before I listened to that inner voice and went out looking for his ass—swollen feet or not.

AMARI

I woke up the next morning and realized I had stayed out for the entire night. I had at least ten missed calls from Tanisha.

I got up and went into the bathroom to wash my face and brush my teeth. I walked back in the bedroom where Kindrah was still sleeping. I kissed her on her cheek and let myself out so that I could go home and face the madness that I was sure was waiting on me.

I couldn't stop thinking about the night I had shared with Kindrah. It was good. It was so good that I wanted to stay and make her some breakfast. I knew if I didn't leave while she was asleep, she would have felt some kind of way about me leaving her after having sex to run back home to Tanisha.

Kindrah gave me more than enough time to leave Tanisha, and I still hadn't had the guts to leave her pregnant with twins. I'm not going to lie; I was really conflicted about the whole situation. On one hand, I wanted to be with Kindrah, but just the thought of leaving Tanisha while she was pregnant with my babies kept me right where I was.

KINDRAH

I couldn't believe Amari left without waking me up. I looked over to see if he left money on the nightstand because that's how I was feeling—like a fucking trick. How the fuck could he do some shit like that to me, of all people, his friend before anything else? I knew he didn't belong to me, and I would have understood if he had to go, but to just leave? Wow.

My feeling were hurt, but I wasn't about to let Amari get me back into a funk about him. Yeah, I loved him. And yes, the dick was good, but hell if I went back to that place I was a couple of months before.

I decided to text Antwan to see what he was doing.

Kindrah: Hey, Mr. Dimples. Are you busy?

Antwan: No, I was waiting on you to hit me up. I've been thinking about you.

Kindrah: Oh really? And what were you thinking?

Antwan: Thinking of when I would see you again.

Kindrah: You will see me at work on Monday. LOL.

Antwan: Oh, you got jokes, I see. I'm talking outside of work, smarty pants.

Kindrah: Well, how about tonight? I'm not busy.

Antwan: Okay, that's cool. Let's chill at my crib. Dinner and an old movie flick . . . if that's okay? If not, we can hit up the movie theatre if you don't feel comfortable coming to the crib.

Kindrah: That's cool. Hit me with the address and time, and I will see you tonight, Mr. Dimples.

I decided to go and get a pedicure, manicure, and something different done to my hair for my date that night. It was a sad situation that I didn't have a girlfriend to call and hang out with me to do those things. It had always been me and Amari doing everything together. I didn't feel comfortable asking him to come with me because the friendship had become complicated. Antwan was a much-needed distraction.

ANTWAN

Monday morning came too fast. I had a great weekend. Spending time with Kindrah was a whole lot of fun. She came over to the house, and we watched Clint Eastwood in *The Good, The Bad, and The Ugly*. I was kind of impressed. I never had a chick who wanted to watch a movie from my old movie collection. When she got there, I had told her to pick a movie while I popped the popcorn, and she picked my favorite movie.

I was really feeling her, and she was beginning to open up to me a little more. She told me about her ex, and she told me that she had a male best friend. I didn't know how to feel about that, but being she had no family, he was basically her only family. Because I wanted to get to know her better, I would have to accept it for now.

I looked up just in time to see her arriving at work. She looked good in her black pants suit, very professional. We worked at the Department of Social Services. We were both supervisors, so we had to keep our dating on the low from nosey coworkers who were always hating, and especially from the females who were always trying to get with a brother.

We made eye contact. She smiled and kept it moving, so I decided to shoot her a quick text.

Antwan: Good Morning, Ms. Kindrah. Looking good this morning.

Kindrah: I look good every morning, Mr. Dimples.

Antwan: I can't argue with that! Talk to you later, sexy lady.

Kindrah: Thanks, Mr. Dimples. Later.

That woman was going to have me falling in love. She was so damn sexy and down to earth, and that was so hard to find these days.

AMARI

Amari: Hey, Kindrah, I just want to apologize for the way I left the house without saying bye.

Kindrah: It's cool. I don't regret what happened between us, but I meant what I said about us just being friends. It's clear you're where you want to be, and truth be told, I started seeing someone.

Amari: Well if you started seeing someone and didn't want to have anything with me, why did you sleep with me? Now you're kicking this friend shit. You said you were going to give me some time to make things right, but now you're seeing someone else? Wow.

Kindrah: Amari, it's been months. How long do you think I should wait? Oh, maybe until the twins are grown? SMH. I'm not willing to do that. We said that we will not let this come between our friendship if it didn't work out, and it didn't work out. I want us to continue being friends, and I would like for you to meet Antwan

Amari: I see you done fell and bumped your head. It's not going to happen. I'm out.

Kindrah: Wow. So all that "we will still be friends" talk was bullshit? Well, be out. I still love you, friend. LOL.

Amari: So not funny. Love you too. Later.

KINDRAH

I got home and fixed me a turkey and cheese sandwich on whole wheat and had some apple juice. Just as I sat in front of the television to watch a movie, the doorbell rang. To my surprise, it was Amari.

"Why didn't you just let yourself in like you did last time?" I asked.

"I didn't know if you had company or not, so I rang the bell," he answered with attitude.

I walked back over to the sofa and continued eating my sandwich. Amari tried to act as if he was watching TV, but I could see him watching me. He clearly had something on his mind and didn't know how to express it as he sat there biting on his bottom lip.

So I asked him, "Why you staring at me but not saying anything?"

And that's when he hit me with the bullshit. "So you really seeing someone else?" he asked.

Guys kill me. I was his for the taking. He tiptoed around the situation, and now he wanted to cock block because I decided to stop chasing his ass.

"I just have one question. Where does this leave us?" he asked.

"Amari, we're going to continue to be friends, and like I said, I met someone. I would like you to meet him and feel him out for me so I know if I should pursue something with him or move on."

"So you're really serious about dude?"

"Yes, I am," I said.

Now that Amari saw that I was not trying to hear his ass, he wanted to sit with his little attitude. I got up, put my dish in the sink, and proceeded up the stairs to take a shower. I was so done stressing over Amari's selfish ass.

Oh, hell no! I got out of the shower and this fool was in my bed! I sat on the edge of the bed and faced him.

"Amari, on some real shit, why are you playing with my feelings? We agreed that if it didn't work out, we would continue to be friends. It didn't work out. I waited and waited on you to do what you said you were going to do to no avail. I poured my heart out to you. I even gave myself to you, and still no commitment. You think you can continue to sell me a dream, and when I'm trying to move on and be happy, you're hating."

I didn't realize how much it really bothered me that we weren't together until I felt the hot tears running down my face.

"Look, Kindrah, I'm not trying to lead you on. I meant every word that I said to you. I love you, and I want to be with you, but it's not as easy as you think. You know I'm a stand-up dude, and it's hard walking away while she's carrying my twins."

"I know, Amari. That's why I let you off the hook, and I'm trying to move on. I knew it would be hard for you to just walk away. You're not built like that. As much as it hurts me not to be with you the way I need to, I'm willing to continue to just be friends. Continuing to sleep together is only going to complicate things even more," I said.

The waterworks were really coming down now. Amari grabbed me and held me in his arms. He rocked me back and forth and asked me not to cry, but I only cried harder. He began kissing my tears, and he slowly begin to kiss my lips, slipping his tongue into my mouth. My better judgment was telling me no, but my love for him and my body were on the same page as I tongued him back. I was already naked under my towel, so he continued to kiss me down below.

Better judgment lost the battle. We slowly made love and drifted off to sleep. I woke up to my cell phone alerting me that I had a text message.

Antwan: What time are we on for tonight?
Kindrah: What time is good for you?
Antwan: I will pick you up at 8 p.m.
Kindrah: Okay, that works for me. See you later.

I know what you're thinking: *Didn't you just get finished sleeping with Amari?* Well, yes I did, but I was not about to let Amari mess up what may be a future with Antwan.

AMARI

As I lay there in bed, I saw Kindrah texting on her phone, smiling and shit. I was not about to lose her to the next dude. I had to pull the plug on this little romance before it got out of hand. I was also going to have to let Tanisha know that after the twins were born, I wanted to be in their lives, but Kindrah was who I wanted to be with.

I cleared my throat to let Kindrah know that I was up. She walked over and sat on the bed. I looked her in the eyes and told her she meant the world to me and that I really did love her. I then told her that I was going to tell Tanisha that night that I was leaving.

She didn't look convinced, so I kissed her lips to let her know that I was serious. We sealed the deal by sexing the rest of the morning. We showered then went to IHOP for breakfast.

After dropping Kindrah back at home, I left to deal with Tanisha, saying a silent prayer that all went well. I had to come up with another excuse because I told her that I had stayed at my cousin's house the night that I spent with Kindrah and didn't come home. I couldn't say that shit again because she spoke to my cousin's girlfriend and found out that I wasn't at his house. I was just going to tell her that I stayed at my father's house to get my mind clear before telling her that I wanted to be with Kindrah.

I was biting on my bottom lip before I even made it to the house. I needed to find a way to tell her this shit without her getting all crazy on me.

TANISHA

"I can't believe Amari. Why doesn't he understand I love him?" I screamed as I injected myself with Pitocin to induce my labor.

I had threatened my friend's husband, who was a labor and delivery doctor, that if he didn't give me the drug, I would tell his wife that we'd been having an affair and that my babies were his. He panicked, even though he knew my babies weren't his. He had been intimate with me on a few occasions and only found out how crazy I was after the fact. All he could think of was his wife believing that he had an affair and taking him for half of everything he had accomplished in the last five years.

I started having mild contractions. I was so desperate that I went against the doctor's instructions on the usage. Injecting myself again, I doubled over in pain as I dialed Amari's number, telling him I was in labor. He sounded like he was panicking as he told me he was on his way.

I delivered Tiara Monae James, six pounds twelve ounces, and Tiana Janae James, five pounds six ounces. Surprisingly, both babies were born without any complications. I was exhausted.

I sat watching Amari as he stared at his babies. He was in love and couldn't wait to take them home. He called Kindrah to let her know that I had delivered the babies early, which wasn't uncommon with twins. Before calling her, he asked me if it was okay if she came to visit the twins, and I told him that I didn't mind. I would love to see the look on her face when she saw my babies, who looked just like their daddy. She told him that she would come the next day on her lunch break.

Amari's family was at the hospital, and I couldn't wait for them to leave because I hadn't been to sleep since the twins were delivered. Amari was staying with me at the hospital that night, and I was thankful because I knew as soon as I closed my eyes, I wouldn't hear the twins if they even attempted to cry. His family finally left, and he was feeding Tiara when I finally dozed off.

KINDRAH

I stopped at the gift shop and bought twin teddy bears for the babies and a "congrats" balloon for Tanisha. When I walked in the room, Tanisha had this look on her face. It wasn't a look of hate, but a look of, *Yeah, bitch, I just had his babies. Compete with that.*

I ignored the look, handed her the items, and said congratulations. I walked over to look at the babies, and I'd be lying if I said they weren't gorgeous. Both of them had light brown eyes, skin like their dad's, and shiny black curly hair. I'm not going to lie; I was feeling some kind of way. Looking at Amari's face when he looked at his twins and the twinkle in his eyes when he spoke to Tanisha made me feel as if I wasn't even in the room. I put my game face on and said congrats again. I let him know I had to get back to work, but when I got outside of the hospital, I went straight home, calling my supervisor to let her know I had a family emergency.

Once I reached home, I felt myself getting depressed all over again, but I refused to let one tear fall. I knew all that Amari claimed would happen once the babies were born went out the back door. His eyes had said it all.

I'd been calling him for a few days, getting no answer or any return calls from him. Seeing all of his status updates on Facebook and the pictures of him, the babies, Tanisha, and his father didn't make it any easier.

The latest update had me crying a river. He wrote under a picture of him and Tanisha, each of them holding one of the twins. It read: *My beautiful princesses, Tiara and Tiana, and my soon-to-be wife.* What bothered me the most was the fact that he knew that I was his friend on Facebook, and he had just promised to be with me, so to post the update without coming to let me know to my face really hurt me. I was hurting so bad that I called out sick from work for the rest of the week, even ignoring Antwan's calls and text messages asking me if I was okay.

These last couple of days had been the worst. I had two glasses of Moscato to help me sleep, and as soon as I drifted off, someone was knocking on my door. I grabbed my robe and was shocked to see Amari at the door, looking good enough to eat. I had to focus and remember how he treated me.

"Why are you here, Amari?" I asked with attitude in my voice.

"Can I come in?" he asked, not answering my question.

I moved to the side and allowed him to come in. He sat on the sofa, and I sat on the opposite side.

"Kindrah, I know that I haven't been a friend to you in the last couple of days, and I know that you've been calling and texting, and I never responded. I was a coward, and I didn't want to come by because I didn't want to see the look that you have on your face right now. I know I hurt you when I promised that I would never hurt you again, but when my daughters came into this world and I looked at them, I couldn't imagine not being in their lives and living elsewhere. I also realized that they deserve to be with their mother and father in the same household with the same last name."

I gasped when I realized what he was talking about. I couldn't breathe, and for the life of me, I couldn't understand how this man, who had been my friend and my lover, who said he loved me, could hurt me like this. No discussion, no nothing. Just up and gets engaged. Why didn't I just go with my first thought to leave him alone and only be friends, especially when I found a man who really wanted to be with me, and just me? Now here I was being hurt again by the man who meant the world to me. I wanted to stop the tears, but my heart was hurting all over again. He had the nerve to try to comfort me, and I pulled away, asking him to leave. He looked at me with hurt eyes, but nothing Amari could say or do would ever make me forgive him for this. I had no words for him.

"Just know that I will always love you, and I hope one day you will understand that I did what was best for my daughters," he had the nerve to say as he got up to leave.

The next couple of days I was a mess, drinking and crying myself to sleep. I just wished I could get him out of my system. I was tired of hurting.

Any day now, I was going to lose my job. I really needed to get back to me before I lost myself, crying over a man that never belonged to me to begin with. I showered, did some much-needed cleaning, and decided to text Antwan.

Hey, I just wanted to apologize for shutting you out. I was going through something, and I needed to work it out on my own. I should've given you an explanation, and if you can find it in your heart to let me explain now, it would really mean a lot to me.

A few hours later, and still no response from Antwan, I decided to go to bed. I was tipsy and exhausted from the crying bullshit.

A few days later, I pulled myself together. I was back to work and finally getting Amari out of my system. I started hanging out, getting to know Antwan again.

KINDRAH

I wasn't feeling good one morning. I felt as if I was going to pass out, so I sat on the edge of the bed. I reached over and turned on the fan that sat next to the bed. I started to feel a little better, but when I went to stand, it felt like the room was spinning. I'd had a few glasses of wine the night before when I went out with Robin from my job, but I wasn't drunk and shouldn't have been feeling like this.

I called Robin to tell her I wasn't feeling well. She agreed to stop by to pick me up and drive me to work. I managed to get in the shower and get dressed without incident. I made toast and poured a glass of orange juice while I waited for Robin.

Once we made it to work, I didn't feel any better. I got up to go to the bathroom, and the last thing I remembered was the room spinning and everything fading to black. When I woke up, I was in the hospital. To my left, Antwan was sleeping in the chair beside the window. I tried reaching for the pitcher of water, accidentally knocking it over. Antwan jumped up out of his sleep. I smiled, and he smiled back.

"How you feeling, Ms. Kindrah?" he asked.

"What happened? Why am I in the hospital?" I asked. After my last stay, I never wanted to see another hospital for as long as I lived.

"You fainted at work and you've been in and out of consciousness. You've been here for about a week. The doctors are trying to figure out what is causing you to keep blacking out all of a sudden. You had three episodes on three different occasions."

I couldn't believe what I was hearing. Just when I was getting my life somewhat back to a normal state, this happened.

"Oh, before I forget, Amari was here. He left those flowers and the yellow envelope on the nightstand next to your bed.

I'm going to head out. I will be back tomorrow after work." He kissed me on the cheek and left.

When I looked at the envelope on the night stand, my palms started to sweat. I was so nervous, and my hands were shaking so badly. I sat up and grabbed what was left in the water pitcher, pouring some water while trying to calm my nerves. In that moment, I realized that I was still very much in love with Mr. Amari James, no matter how much I ranted that I hated him.

I pulled the letter out of the envelope and began to read:

> Hey, Kindrah.
> I know I'm the last person you wanted to hear from, but your job called me because I'm your emergency contact. When I got to the hospital, dude from your job was posted up, and I felt some kind of way. I know I really have no reason or right to feel this way, but I should be the one by your side. We have history, and I really hate that our relationship has come to us being strangers. The twins are getting big and haven't even spent time with my best friend, their godmother. We always have been there for each other, but we have let each other down. We promised that we wouldn't let anything tear us apart, and look at us, not even speaking. If you can find it in your heart to reach out and try to restore our friendship, please call me. I know I don't deserve a second chance, but I'm begging you to please think about it.

I couldn't help but smile. I missed him and the friendship we'd shared since we were kids. How do you just throw that away? I was going to call him, but I wouldn't rush it. I would give it some time.

Antwan and I had become closer since the incident. I realized how much he really liked and cared for me. We were hanging out and doing things couples do, but we didn't put a title on it. I'd been home for about a month now, and I was feeling much better.

One night, Antwan and I were going out.

"Where are we going?" I asked.

"Just sit back and relax. I got this." He smiled, showing his deep dimples.

"Okay, Mr. Dimples, if you say so." I smiled, realizing I was happy that I got a second chance with him.

Antwan pulled up to the roller skating rink.

"Are you serious?" I asked, giving him the side eye.

"What? Don't tell me Ms. Kindrah can't skate."

"Who said I can't skate? Did you see that I'm wearing tight-ass jeans and five-inch stilettos?"

"Well, you won't be skating in your heels. We will be wearing skates . . . duh!"

I punched him in his arm for trying to be cute. He smiled his signature smile that I just loved.

We had a great night, even though I fell five times trying to be cute, doing tricks. I really didn't want the night to end. I couldn't remember the last time I just relaxed and enjoyed myself.

"Hey, what you over there thinking about?" he asked.

"I was just thinking that I really enjoyed myself. Thank you for showing me a good time," I answered.

"Anything for you, Ms. Kindrah," he said as he reached over and kissed me lightly on the lips then opened the car door for me.

Once we made it back to my place, I invited him in to continue our night. We decided on drinks and a movie because we had already had dinner at the roller rink. We decided on one of my favorite movies, *Claudine,* a classic in my eyes. We laughed and continued to have a good time. I cuddled up on the sofa in his arms, and at that moment, I didn't want to be anywhere else.

It had been almost two months since Amari left the letter at the hospital. I finally decided to give him a call. He picked up on the first ring.

"Hey, you. How have you been?"

"I've been okay. I was wondering if you wanted to meet up somewhere to talk," I said.

"Can we meet at the park? Because I have the twins with me, and I would really like for you to finally see them again. It's been like forever."

"Okay."

"So how about noon at Wakefield Park, by the swings?" he asked.

"Sounds good. See you there."

After I hung up the phone with Amari, I went to take a shower. I can't lie; I was kind of excited to see him again. Besides, despite all of the madness, we were best friends before anything. I put on a hot pink Dereon halter with matching shorts and a pair of gold sandals to match the gold in the logo. My hair was already in braids, so I put them in a ponytail in front with the back out. I added some eyeliner and some lip gloss, and then I was out the door.

I was kind of nervous as I neared the park. I wanted to turn around, but I decided to just go and get it over with. I was trying to fight the feelings I had about seeing him again.

AMARI

I got the twins dressed in matching shorts sets then put headbands on their heads. I added a little baby oil, and we were good to go. I had on my army fatigue khakis with an army green wife beater, some white socks, and my Jordan flip flops, keeping it simple. I put both of the girls into the truck in their cars seats, and we were on our way.

Once we got to the park, I pulled out the twin stroller, putting both of them in. We walked over to the swing area, where Kindrah was sitting on the bench, reading from her Kindle. She looked so beautiful in her hot pink. She must have felt my presence because she looked up and smiled.

"Oh my God, the twins have gotten so big! They are beautiful. Look at those cheeks," she cooed.

Tania looked at Kindrah and smiled. Tiara just sat there, blowing spit bubbles.

I gave them their bottles to keep them quiet so that Kindrah and I could have a serious talk without any interruptions.

"Okay, let me just say that I'm sorry for hurting you. I know I sound like a broken record, but believe me when I say that I miss you. I'm really sorry that I destroyed the friendship by not being honest with you and letting you find out about me and Tanisha on Facebook. She proposed to me at the hospital. She had the ring and everything. I was so caught up in the moment that I said yes. I felt like my daughters should have both parents with the same last name and residence.

"At that time, that's where I wanted to be. We didn't get married, though," he said, shocking the hell out of me. "Tanisha has really been showing me that she isn't stable, and some of the things that she does makes me a little scared to leave the twins with her. I don't know if it's postpartum depression or not. I have been trying to get her to see a doctor, and she refuses.

"So as of lately, I have been caring for the twins without much help from her. When I work, I leave them with my dad being that he works the day shift and I work the night shift. I have really been going through it with her, and to be honest, I really don't know what else to do. I have threatened to leave her if she didn't agree to get some help, but all my threats fall on deaf ears."

KINDRAH

I couldn't believe what Amari was telling me. I'd heard of postpartum depression, and it did sound like the symptoms of it, but she would leave the house for days and come home like nothing happened. Amari said that when she did have the kids, she yelled at them as if they weren't babies. He said he tried reaching out to her family, but no one was responding to any of his calls.

I mean, I felt bad that he was going through this with Tanisha, but I really didn't know what to say because I still felt some type of way about how he did me. But then I had to ask myself, how could I be selfish in his time of need? Just thinking about all the years of him and his father being there for me started to outweigh any of the things he put me through in the past months.

"I'm still hurt, but I'm not going to lie; not a day goes by that I don't think about you. I miss our friendship more than anything, and I'm willing to put all the bullshit behind us and get back to being friends. If you ever need my help with my godbabies, all you have to do is ask. I really hate that I missed out on so much of their lives already. Since I'm still home on disability, most of my days are spent watching television, bored to death," I said.

"I'm so happy that you're willing to give our friendship another try, and I promise I will never hurt you again. I love you and need you in my life, now more than ever."

He started tearing up, and so did I. We hugged and spent the rest of the afternoon catching up, allowing me time to get to know the twins.

After lunch from the frank truck in the park, we departed and went our separate ways. I felt so much better now that

Amari and I were friends again, but I felt kind of sad about what Tanisha was going through. Even though she and I weren't friends, I still hoped she changed her mind and spoke to someone. The twins needed their mom.

AMARI

Once I made it back to the house, Tanisha still wasn't home, and I was starting to worry. I called around to some of her friends, and no one had heard from her. While I waited, I gave the twins a bath, gave them their bottles for the night, and put them in their cribs. Twenty minutes later, they were both sleeping.

I decided to give Kindrah a call to see what she was doing. She told me that she and Antwan were out having dinner and that she would give me a call back later that evening. I went to the kitchen to fix a drink but headed back to the living room when I heard keys turning in the door. Tanisha walked in, looking as if she hadn't washed in days.

"Tanisha, where the hell have you been?" I asked her.

She looked at me, rolled her eyes, and then sat on the couch.

"Tanisha, I know you hear me talking to you. Your ass left here, and you didn't think to call or nothing? You had me worried."

"Well, you don't have to worry about me. I'm fine. Last time I checked, I was grown," she said.

I wanted to slap some sense into her so bad. I really didn't understand what the hell was going on with her, and I was really getting tired of trying to figure it out.

"Yes, you're grown, but you have two kids who you have yet to assist me with. They need their mother. I need to know what the hell is going on with you. I told you if you're having postpartum depression, I will go with you to the doctor to see what we can do to help you. But right now, this leaving for days, sometimes weeks . . . I can't do this anymore. I can't be all stressed out while taking care of the girls, so you let me know right now if you're going to let me help you get the help you need. If not, the girls and I are going to stay with my dad.

That way I don't have to be going back and forth from his house to our place."

When I said that, she flipped as she turned the table over, sending all of the picture frames crashing to the floor.

"Let me tell you one motherfucking thing. I don't give a fuck how you feel about what I do. Like I told you, I'm grown, and I will continue to do as I please. I don't need your help because there isn't shit wrong with me. I need a damn break from you and these damn kids. Is that too much to ask?"

I just stood there in shock. What happened to her? This was not the Tanisha that I loved and knew, but one thing that I did know was if she refused to get help, I was leaving in the morning. I was going to get a few of my things and the girls' things and go to my dad's house. All I could do was try to contact her family again, and hopefully someone responded so I could let them know that she needed to get help. I couldn't have my girls going through this with her.

I walked away from her to go upstairs and tend to the twins because she woke them up when she sent the table and picture frames flying across the room. When I got the girls back down, I walked back downstairs to try to talk to Tanisha for the last time, but she had already left the house.

It had been a few weeks now that I was staying with my dad. I finally got in touch with Tanisha's mother, and I couldn't believe that Tanisha had lied to me all these years. Her mother stated that Tanisha had been diagnosed with bipolar disorder when she turned fifteen years old. Her mother also told me that she was always a troubled child, but when she got to high school, she began to have violent outbursts. When she was evaluated and started to see a psychologist, she received treatment and medication. She stated that as long as she was on her medication, she was okay. She also said that once Tanisha reached adulthood, they moved to Georgia and tried to get her to move with them, but she refused.

I was in a complete state of shock. I thought back on some of the things she would say or do in the relationship and realized that the signs had been there. I called my uncle, who was a psychologist. He informed me that childbirth could have triggered her manic behavior. I told him that she refused to go to the doctor, and he told me to be careful and not to leave her alone with the children.

When I say that my head was banging, I mean it felt like it would explode at any second. If I'd had Tylenol in my hand, I would have taken the whole damn bottle.

I didn't have to work that night, so once I finished getting the girls dressed, we were on our way to Kindrah's place for the night. She was the one who had kept me sane through it all, because I felt like I was losing my mind dealing with Tanisha.

KINDRAH

I finished cooking dinner and was waiting for Amari and the twins to arrive. While I was waiting, I decided to give Antwan a call. I told him about Amari and the twins spending the night, and he wasn't happy about it. I reminded him that Amari was my best friend and nothing else. I felt kind of bad not telling him about our sexual relationship, but I didn't want to ruin what we had already repaired. I talked to him for about twenty minutes.

Amari and the twins got to my house at about 7:30 that evening. After we got the twins washed and in their pajamas, Amari fed Tania and I fed Tiara. We put them down in their portable bassinets.

I fixed our plates, and we sat at the table. Amari filled me in on the recent dealings with Tanisha, and all I could say was "Wow." I really didn't know what else to say. He looked so stressed and like he had aged overnight. I suggested that he take some aspirin and lay down, and I would get the twins if they woke up. He agreed.

We sat and watched *The Hangover* until he dozed off. I shook him lightly and told him he could go sleep in the guest room, but he didn't budge. I went and got a blanket out of the closet, covered him with it, and continued to watch my movie.

My phone beeped. I had a text message from Antwan.

Antwan: Hey baby girl. What you doing?

Kindrah: Watching The Hangover while Amari and the twins are sleeping.

Antwan: Do you want some company? I promise not to fall asleep on you. LOL

Kindrah: He didn't fall asleep on me. He has a lot going on. He took some aspirin and tried to stay up, but he couldn't. And you can keep me company tomorrow night and we can watch The Hangover Part 2 together.

Antwan: That's cool. So tomorrow it is. Have a good night, and sweet dreams.

Kindrah: Thanks, and you have a good night, too. Thanks for being so understanding.

Antwan: I trust you, baby girl.

After I finished texting with Antwan, I looked over and saw that Amari was awake.

"Hey, sleepy head. You feel any better?" I asked.

"I feel a little better. So what's up with you and this dude? Is it serious?"

"Well, right now, we're just hanging out. We really didn't put any title to what we have, but I will say that I like him a lot and hope that it develops to be much more."

"Well, you deserve to be happy, and if dude makes you happy, then you should let him know how you feel," he said.

"I thought about it, but look what happened when I told the last dude how I felt," I said, laughing.

"Oh, I see you got jokes! Anyway, what's up with the movie?"

"Oh, you mean the movie you fell asleep on?"

"Well, I'm up now. Start it over."

"Oh, hell no. You better put another movie in. I'm not about to watch the same one again," I said.

He got up and put in *Think Like a Man*. I got up to use the bathroom and to get something to drink.

I was awakened out of my sleep. At first I thought I was dreaming, but once Tania started screaming like someone was killing her, I jumped up. Amari didn't even attempt to get up. I picked her up and tried to get her quiet before she woke Tiara up. I warmed her bottle and was feeding her when Tiara started screaming. I guess this was the time of morning when they ate. I rocked Tiara's bassinet with my foot to quiet her down while I finished feeding Tania.

After I was done feeding Tiara, both girls were quiet. I sat both of them in the twin stroller and put *Dora the Explorer* on the television. I went upstairs to wash my face and brush my teeth, and then fixed breakfast for me and Amari. I set the table then woke his behind up and told him to go get cleaned up because breakfast was ready. When he saw the twins up watching TV, he thanked me.

It was crazy how a couple of months ago, I would have given anything to have Amari and be the mother of his twins, but I could honestly say that it felt good to just have my friend back. Since I had really gotten to know Antwan, he was who I want to be with, and I hoped for the life of me that he could really accept my friendship with Amari. I really would hate to have to choose.

TANISHA

I didn't know if I was coming or going, but I knew that I needed to get back on my medication. I constantly had crazy thoughts and did crazy things, but I usually knew what I was doing when I was doing it. Since the twins had been born, I'd been doing things that didn't even make sense to me, like I had no control over who I hurt and why I hurt them.

I hadn't seen the twins in so long, and Amari had basically given up on me. I knew he was just trying to protect the babies, but he shouldn't have just up and left me like that. Yeah, I refused his help, but shit, he should've kept trying. Instead, he just packed up my babies and left me.

The place was a mess, and so was I. I didn't know when was the last time I washed or even combed my hair. I had seen my aunt the week before, the one that didn't give a shit about me, and she had the nerve to tell me that I really needed to get some help. I slapped that bitch so hard that I thought I broke her neck. I had to run because once she fell to the ground, someone called the ambulance. They should have left her ass laying there. She had some damn nerve to judge me. Who the hell did she think she was, telling me I'm a mother now and I needed to act as such? Didn't she think I knew that? And for her information, I was going to get my babies back, and Amari had better not try to stop me, or he'd be very fucking sorry.

Bang! Bang! Bang!

I was snapped out of my thoughts as I heard someone knocking on the door like the fucking police. At first I thought I was dreaming, but I heard it again. This time it was harder. I didn't even realize I had dozed off.

I jumped up to answer the door. I was shocked to be looking at both of my parents, standing there looking at me with stunned expressions on their faces.

AMARI

Tanisha's parents had just left from seeing the twins for the first time. They told me that they managed to get Tanisha in to see her old doctor, who was a friend of Tanisha's dad. He agreed to treat her. They also informed me that they would be taking her back to Georgia with them until she was stable again. Her mom said that she would like for Tanisha to be able to visit with the twins before they left in the next couple of days, with supervision, of course. She also told me that her and her husband cleaned up the apartment that Tanisha and I shared, and then she handed me a notebook. It was Tanisha's journal. She made me promise that for the sake of the twins that I wouldn't give the book to the authorities. She was only giving it to me-so that I would have some type of understanding as to why they were taking her home.

After reading Tanisha's journal, all I could do was thank God that Kindrah and the twins were spared. Yes, Kindrah had endured a lot at the hands of Tanisha, but I was thankful she still had her life. For the life of me, I couldn't really understand how I was with Tanisha for three years and had no clue that she had a mental illness. I loved her, but I knew that Tanisha and I would never be together again, not only for my safety, but for the safety of my daughters and my best friend.

I put the notebook in the shredder. I made a promise to her mother, and there wasn't anything that jail could do for Tanisha. She needed treatment, and jail was no place to get her the help that she needed. I decided to put it in God's hands, and I also decided that I wouldn't even share this information with Kindrah. I prayed for all the victims who had lost their lives.

AMARI

As I sat and watched the eleven o'clock news, nothing could have prepared me for what the anchorman announced:

"A Georgia husband and wife, who have been identified as Tammy and Gerald Watkins, were found murdered in their home early this evening. Their deaths are being ruled a homicide, and authorities are looking to question the couple's only child, Tanisha Watkins. Next door neighbors reported seeing Tanisha leaving the residence after hearing arguing."

I was in a state of shock as I stared at the television, and for some reason, I felt the need to check on the twins. As I turned to go upstairs, I was startled upon seeing Tanisha, standing near the stairs with a gun in her hand and a crazed look in her eyes.

I stood still for a few seconds, staring at Tanisha. I couldn't believe that she would be responsible for killing her parents. You really have to be some kind of sick to kill your own parents. Then again, I really didn't know why I was in shock at this point because it wasn't like she hadn't killed before. The part I was having a hard time with was why she would kill her own parents.

Tania started crying, but Tanisha didn't budge from standing near the stairs.

"Tanisha, what are you doing here?" I asked.

I repeated myself three times, and Tanisha just stood there, looking at me like she was in shock. Once I saw that she wasn't there to harm me, I slowly walked over to her and removed the gun from her hands. She continued standing there with a deranged look in her eyes and not speaking.

Not knowing what to do, I called my uncle, who had given me advice on her condition a while back. Being that he was a psychologist, who better to tell me what to do with the situation at hand? He told me to call 911 and brief them on the situation, but to make sure I told them that she was non-responsive.

After the dispatcher told me that EMS had been notified and they were en route, I hung up the phone and waited for them to arrive. For some strange reason, I felt the need to protect her, so I hid the gun.

When the authorities arrived, Tanisha still wasn't speaking. She didn't respond to any of the EMT's questions. I overheard the EMT tell the officers that she was in shock. An officer briefed the emergency unit on the situation, and Tanisha was placed under arrest, even though she didn't respond to what was being said. She was read her rights, and they handcuffed her right hand onto the gurney.

The EMTs told me that she was under arrest, but she was being taken to Bellevue Hospital to be evaluated. I called Kindrah to come and stay with the twins so that I could go up to the hospital. I was worried, and I also needed to find out what was going to happen to her.

I got all the way up to the hospital just to be told that she was under arrest and on a 72-hour hold. She wasn't allowed any visitors until after she was arraigned and formally charged. The officer told me that she was going to be arraigned sometime the next morning from her hospital bed. He also told me that once she was put into the system, I could either go online or call the number on the card he handed me to get her case and booking numbers. Once I got the booking number, I would be able to find out what her charges were, and if she would be able to post bail.

I didn't know if they were going to be charging her for Kindrah's accident, but what I did know was that after her 72-hour hold, if they said she was okay to travel, the Georgia authorities were going to be there to extradite her right back there to face murder charges.

Once I got back into the house, Kindrah was sitting on the couch, with her legs folded under her, eating ice cream.

"Hey, how did it go?" she asked.

"Well, I got all the way to the hospital just for them to tell me she couldn't have visitors."

"I'm really in shock. Who would've guessed that Tanisha was capable of murder? I mean, I know she's been dealing with mental issues, but murder? It's really hard to believe. And for her to be accused of killing her own parents . . . I can't begin to think of any reason that would make a person kill their own parents."

"I'm not sure if she's capable of murder, Kindrah. I'm just as shocked as you."

"Well, I know this is unexpected, and you might not be up to it, but we have to start planning my godbabies' first birthday party."

I looked at Kindrah like she was crazy. Tania and Tiara's mother was being charged with murder. Why in the hell would I be thinking about a damn birthday party hours after my kids' mother was arrested? I really felt like going in on her for even saying some stupid shit like that, but I didn't.

"Kindrah, I doubt I will be celebrating the twins' birthday. I have to concentrate on what's going to happen to Tanisha. I'm stressed about the whole situation as it is, so right now, that's my first priority."

"Okay, cool. I'm going to head out. Call me if you need me." She grabbed her bag and left.

I didn't know what had just happened, but she was acting really strange. I didn't have time to address it. This Tanisha shit had me stressed the fuck out, real talk.

I locked the door and sat on the couch with my head in my hands. I had a lot going on. I didn't know if Tanisha was going to be charged with Kindrah's accident. If she did get charged and Kindrah found out that the officers already told me that she was a suspect, I knew for sure our friendship was going to be over.

I got up to fix a much-needed drink. I didn't know what to do. If I told Kindrah and then Tanisha wasn't charged, I would end up losing our friendship for nothing. But if I didn't tell her and Tanisha was charged, and she found out I knew all along, I would lose our friendship for lying. I was giving myself a headache with the back and forth of a situation that didn't make any sense to me. I decided to just to leave it alone for now.

KINDRAH

I couldn't believe Amari looked me right in my face and lied. I gave him the opportunity to come clean and to be honest with me. I was so tired of people who claimed to love me always ending up hurting me. It was really starting to do something to my mental.

I can't lie; when Officer Creer came to visit me and informed me that Tanisha was the person responsible for my accident, I was shocked. Officer Creer said that they were able to locate her from the address that was on file for her at the Department of Motor Vehicles.

Officer Creer expressed her surprise because she remembered Amari being at the hospital with me the whole time. She was kind of confused that Amari's girlfriend would be responsible for hurting his best friend, and she asked me if there was anything going on with me and Amari. I told her no because at the time of my accident, there wasn't anything going on, so I really didn't have any answers for why Tanisha would want to hurt me.

She said that they told Amari they had reason to believe Tanisha was responsible for my accident and wanted her to come in for questioning. Amari told her that he had no idea of Tanisha's whereabouts. That proved to me who he loved more, and I was going to show him who I loved more. Right now, I was going to pretend everything was cool, but he would soon find out he hurt me one time too many. I was no longer the same Kindrah. She had been replaced.

I had to let Antwan's ass go, too, because he was another one who had been with me for a year, and as soon as I gave him my prized possession, the games started. He stopped answering and returning my calls, basically just playing the mind games that men play. Who stays with someone a whole year just to get some ass? Where they do that at? I knew men that get the ass then bounce, but an entire year was unheard of. The part that bothered me the most was that he was up at the job messing around with another supervisor. Since I was still out on medical leave, all my information was confirmed by my girl, Robin, so he didn't have to worry about me ever calling his ass again. Not that he was answering anyway.

I finally started using the insurance money I got from my parents. I had been looking for a new place but had yet to find something that I liked. I did finally upgrade my car to the new Range Rover, fully loaded, and I loved it. I also started hanging out and finally had some female friends. Who would have guessed I would have friends? It felt foreign at first because I never had any real friends besides Amari. He caused me so much pain and heartache that I ended up having trust issues; I didn't know who was a friend or foe. I really didn't know how to accept that someone really wanted to be my friend without wanting something in return, but I put that fear behind me and just started doing me. I was enjoying life and playing by my rules.

SHELBY

"Oh God, Dre. Why are you always into this freaky shit?"

"Babe, just relax. I'm not going to drop you."

I couldn't believe I let this nigga talk me into going out on the fucking balcony. He convinced me to sit my big ass on the cold damn railing on the tenth floor while he sucked on my pussy.

"Shell, you can't grab my head like that. You better hold on to the rail before your ass falls," he said.

"Dre. Oh God, put me down! Oooh, this shit feels so good." I held on to the rail as I lifted my butt up like I was doing butt crunches, fucking his face. It didn't take me long to cum as my body relaxed.

Dre carefully helped me down, just to bend my ass over the balcony table to fuck the shit out of me. I was hoping like hell that I wasn't giving the neighbors in the building across the street another show.

I found out the next day that we had in fact been on display. The Tenant Association went ham on my ass in a memo. The memo stated that at least ten families had filed a complaint. One parent even said she caught her son watching my freak show. I already had two prior warnings for inappropriate behavior.

Dre thought the shit was so funny, but I told his ass if I got kicked out of my condo, my ass would be moving in with him. I was really hoping it didn't come to that because he lived in the hood, and I wasn't trying to be living in nobody's hood.

I had never been so embarrassed in my life, going in front of the Tenant Board, trying to explain to them why I was fucking on my balcony and not in the bedroom like normal people. I wanted to tell them that my boyfriend was a fuck-anywhere type of dude, and I couldn't help but oblige whenever he requested the pussy, but I didn't. I apologized and told those stuck-up, no-getting-dick bitches it would never happen again.

After Dre and I got out of the shower, we had to get ready to head out to the club to meet up with Kindrah and the rest of the crew. This would be Dre's first time meeting Kindrah, but he knew everyone else. We were going to Club Envy for the night, a new club on the lower east side. Dre sweated out my hair, so I had to get my shit back right before I went anywhere. I couldn't believe I let him fuck up my hair when I just paid a buck to get the shit done.

"Shell, how a nigga look?"

I just stared at his ass. My boo was so fucking fine. He had on some black True Religion jeans, a black True Religion button down, and some Steve Maddens on his feet. My baby stood at six one, two hundred ten pounds of sexiness, with light brown eyes, a smooth bald head, and a goatee trimmed to perfection. He was the shit, and he knew it.

"Babe, you know your ass is always on point," I told him.

"I know, but I got to ask my baby how a nigga looking."

"Nah, you just want to hear me say how sexy your ass looks." I laughed.

"True. Come here and let me hit it real quick," he said, grabbing me from behind.

"Dre, stop. You know I still got to curl my hair because of your ass always wanting to get the pussy before we go out, and I still got to get dressed."

"I'm gonna let you slide, only because I jacked your hair up wearing that ass out," he said, releasing me.

When I came down the stairs a while later, Dre was sitting on the couch with a glass of Hennessy on the table, blazing as always. He must have felt my presence because he turned around, looking at me with lust-filled eyes.

"Damn, Shell. Where you think you going with that shit on?"

I was rocking a sexy black jumpsuit with a high-neck design, mesh panels that showed off skin at the thighs and the breast area, and a pair of black, peep-toe, platform stilettos. My hair was in bouncy curls, and I applied some light makeup and lip gloss. Yeah, I was the shit, and I felt good.

"Dre, don't start."

"Nah, fuck that. Your ass is going to have me fighting dudes all fucking night with you wearing that outfit."

"I'm with you, boo. That's all that matters. A nigga can drool all night, and it wouldn't matter to me because my sexy ass belongs to your sexy ass."

KINDRAH

I had a good time hanging out with the crew, and I must say Shelby's man Dre was a fine specimen. He had my pussy pulsating just looking at his ass. I was sorry Shelby didn't have the pleasure of knowing me when I was a good girl because now that I was a bad girl, Kindrah got what Kindrah wanted, and right about now, I wanted Dre on his knees and in between my legs. I was done waiting on a nigga to love me, and I was definitely done playing nice.

Amari had called to let me know that Tanisha was indicted and charged with murder in the first degree for the deaths of her parents. She still wasn't speaking, so just like he thought, the Georgia authorities picked her up and she was moved to a Georgia psychiatric center. It was a maximum security hospital where she would receive residential treatment and remain there until she was stable enough to stand trial.

Amari was upset that she wouldn't be able to have visits for the first three months. I convinced him to have the twins' first birthday party to try to get his mind off of the situation, even if only for a day. I even told him I would handle everything, and all he would have to do was show up with the twins. He agreed.

I invited Drama and Kimora over to help me plan the party for my goddaughters. It didn't take me long to find a place to have the party, and I booked the space and paid online. I felt it would have been easier to just create the event on Facebook, but most of Amari's family members didn't have accounts. We had to sit and do the invitations the old fashioned way, writing out invitations and putting them in envelopes. I didn't have any stamps, so I would have to make a trip to the post office the next morning to mail them out.

Drama came from the kitchen with some glasses and my bottle of pink Moscato. "Okay, grab a glass and drink up. I'm going to need for the both of you to be good and tipsy to hear this bullshit I'm about to share," Drama said.

"I'm going to need a blunt. They don't call your ass Drama for nothing," Kimora said, laughing.

"Anyway, I get a call today from my homegirl, Trish, telling me this bitch, Hartley told her she's pregnant by TJ. Mind you, this bitch is supposed to be my friend. I know TJ and I have been broken up for two years now, and I don't care that we both have moved on. The bitch still didn't come to me like a fucking woman and tell me the foul shit she did. I just hope I don't go ham on this dumb bitch and get locked up. I'm telling you, bitches are mad foul and disrespectful. To think I made this bitch my son's godmother when I knew she was nothing but a fucking ho."

I was sitting there listening to Drama go off about her friend fucking her baby's father. Mind you, I hadn't known them very long or the history, but I was like, *So fucking what? You and dude haven't been together in mad years, so what's the big fucking deal?* I wanted to tell the bitch to get over it, but I didn't. I just told her she needed to approach the bitch and that sorry-ass baby daddy of hers for crossing that line.

"It really hurts to find out someone who claimed to be my friend could really do something like that to me, even after knowing what his ass put me through. With all that, she still goes, fucks him, and gets pregnant. I can't believe a bitch is that hard up for some dick. I knew she was a ho, but I didn't think the bitch would pull a ho move on me."

"Drama, don't cry. It's not even worth crying over. I know you're hurt because you befriended her and you had her all up in your life, treating the bitch like family."

"Kimora, that's the reason it hurts so much. And on top of being hurt, I feel stupid. I bet they been fucking since the first time I had him drop our son off to her ass. I don't care who approached who. Both of them are wrong for this shit."

"I understand, but don't beat yourself up about it. Karma is a bitch, and they both will get it full circle," I added.

I was so glad when Drama's sister called her to come and pick up her son. Don't get me wrong; I liked them, but all that bullshit they were talking about was getting on my nerves. I really couldn't understand what the problem was. If they hadn't been together for two years, what's the problem?

I finished off the rest of the Moscato, showered, and got in bed. I called Amari to let him know the details of the party. When I hung up, my head hit the pillow, and I was out.

The next day, I got to the post office early. I was in and out since it wasn't crowded. As I was leaving the post office, I saw Dre leaning up against his ride. I started walking off like I didn't see him.

"Oh, so you going to walk by like you don't know a nigga?" he said.

"Do I know you?" I said, fucking with him.

"So you're going to act like I didn't get those panties wet the other night?"

"Somebody's panties, but not mine." My ass was lying. My fucking panties were moist just talking to his ass now, but he didn't need to know that.

"I bet those joints dripping right now." He laughed.

"I think I hear Shelby calling you."

"Yeah, okay. Anyway, what you about to get into?"

"I'm going to get my hair and nails done. Why?"

"Put my number in your phone and hit me up later," he said.

I put his number in my iPhone, trying not to act thirsty.

"Okay, I'm out. My man's across the street waiting on a nigga."

And with that, he thug-walked across the street, and I went to my ride, smiling all the way.

AMARI

I had just finished getting the twins ready for their birthday party. My cousin came earlier to do their hair and helped me get them dressed. She had my babies looking like two little beauty queens. All I had to do was put the tiaras on their heads, put their coats on, and we were ready to roll out. I put them in the truck and waited for my friend, Kelsey, to pull up. Kelsey had been my well-kept secret with all the stress I had been dealing with. I felt I needed her there with me that day because she had been a much-needed distraction.

Once we got to Jimbo's Bouncy Room, I was impressed. At first I was a little worried. Because the twins just started walking, I felt that having a party at a bounce house would be a bit much for them. To my surprise, Kindrah had mini bounce houses and a small track area set up with V-Tech Learning Walkers for the children that had just started walking. She also had those cages with the balls for the older children. The room was decorated in lavender and pink décor. It was so beautiful.

"Oh my God, look at my godbabies looking like little princesses! You both look so cute with your big girl ponytails. Aww! My babies are growing up so fast," Kindrah said.

"Oh, my bad. Kindrah, this is Kelsey; Kelsey, this is Kindrah, my best friend and the twins' godmother," I said.

KINDRAH

Hold the fuck up. Who is this bitch, and where did she come from?

Just that quick, my whole fucking attitude changed. I knew Amari didn't bring no bitch to my godbabies' birthday party without asking me or even giving me the heads up that he was seeing someone. I looked at her and smiled a phony smile because I really wasn't feeling this bitch. I picked up my godbabies and walked off.

I did everything in my power to keep my attitude at bay so that Tania and Tiara enjoyed themselves, as well as the guests, but to watch Amari interact with this bitch pissed me off. Then when he called her Kells I almost lost it. This motherfucker had a nickname for this bitch. *Friend? Yeah, right.*

Yes, he was on my shit list, but I still loved him. He was outright showing her affection, which tugged at my heart just a little. I tried telling myself to get it together. *No more being weak. Fuck love, and fuck every nigga that was not trying to love you.* That little pep talk didn't work, because I felt like going in a corner and crying.

The party went really well considering the funk I was in. When it was time to sing *Happy Birthday*, Drama brought out the birthday cake.

"Who's the plain Jane with Amari?" she whispered in my ear.

"Some friend of his, so he says."

Drama knew of the history with me and Amari because when I first met her, I told her about him. I left out the part about me going off the deep end, the accident, and me still loving him.

After all the kids ate cake and ice cream, I gave out the party bags, and the party was officially over. I was really tired.

I helped Drama take the gifts out to Amari's truck, while Kelsey took Tania and Amari carried Tiara out and put them in their car seats. Amari thanked me and Drama for everything, and he and his friend left.

When I started my ride, my destination was home, but somehow I ended up at Amari's. I saw a BMW parked in the yard, and I assumed it was Kelsey's car, so I tried to wait her out. After sitting in my car for almost an hour and her still not coming out, I figured she was spending the night. I got so upset that I slashed all of her tires in a rage. I jumped in my ride and cried all the way home.

I couldn't call Shelby to vent because I fucked her man and had plans on fucking him again. It was only right to keep my distance. I knew she felt some type of way because I didn't invite her to my goddaughters' birthday party, but I didn't feel like looking her in the face after fucking Dre.

His ass was a bonafide freak. I never met one of them before. He ate the pussy right in the parking lot of the Walmart. We went to buy condoms and ended up fucking in the parking lot against the hood of his ride. I never did no shit like that, but just the fear of someone coming out and seeing us made it so much better.

AMARI

The twins were finally down for the count. They had really enjoyed themselves at the party. I stepped out to walk Kells to her car, and we noticed that her tires were slashed. I panicked a little. Who would slash her tires? Tanisha was all the way in Georgia, so I knew it had nothing to do with me. I had already gone through so much in the past year, and I didn't need to be dealing with no jealousy bullshit from an ex-boyfriend, especially where I lay my head with my daughters. She assured me that she didn't have a crazy ex lurking and trying to get back with her, so now I was really puzzled as to who would do this. Kells called AAA, and they picked the car up.

I didn't want to wake the twins up to drive her home, so she agreed to stay the night in my guest room. After she showered, I gave her one of my T-shirts to put on. We sat on the sofa to watch a movie.

"Amari, can I ask you something?" she said.

"What's up?"

"Did you and Kindrah ever have a relationship?"

"Nah. Why you ask?"

"Because she gave me one of those jealous ex-girlfriend looks," she said, laughing.

"Nah, she's just overprotective of me. She trusts no one, especially around her godbabies. Give it time. She will warm up to you."

Kells and I talked through the whole movie. I couldn't tell you one thing that went on in that movie, but I really enjoyed just sitting and talking, getting to know each other better.

KINDRAH

Today was once again the anniversary of my family's death. I walked into the cemetery with flowers in my hand and tears in my eyes. I had to find the strength to keep walking, no matter how long it had been. This day every year felt as if it had happened yesterday.

As I got closer to my family's final resting place, I saw Amari and the twins standing there, and the tears fell. He walked over, put his arms around me, and I cried for reasons unknown to anyone. After we left the cemetery, we went our separate ways, and he promised to check on me later.

Drama called me later that evening to hang out, but I had to decline. I was meeting up with Dre's fine ass.

I didn't understand how this man had me open. Here we were on a fucking park bench, and I was riding his dick as if common sense didn't exist anymore. His ass started biting my nipples through my shirt, and I went hard, trying to release. Don't get me wrong; I would love this dick in me all night, but my ass was freezing.

Dre didn't seem bothered by this cold New York night in the park. Once we got back to the car, his ass wouldn't let me get in. He had me lean on the hood of the car on my stomach.

"Dre, I'm freezing out here," I said.

"Just give me a minute. Let me taste that ass."

He pulled my jeans and panties down to my ankles and dived in. He was eating my ass with perfection and taking his time. Now, I know a bitch just said her ass was cold, but I wasn't a fool. That shit felt so good. He was a nasty nigga, but I loved it.

When I got home, I showered and took my ass to bed, feeling fulfilled. I should have gotten my ass a side piece a long time ago. I was going bankrupt with all the batteries I had been buying, masturbating like it was going out of style.

I woke up the next day with a stuffy nose, sore throat, and my body hurt all over. That damn Dre. It was his fault, and I probably caught cold in my ass.

I called Amari, and he said he would bring me some soup and some cold medicine. It hurt like hell to move, but that's what my dumb ass got for fucking in the park.

I called Dre's ass and cursed him out. He said he would come through that night, but his ass wasn't coming anywhere near my crib. He was a booty call, and that was the extent of it. I was not trying to fall in love. Amari was still my one and only love.

DRAMA

Why did I get home only to see TJ and Hartley sitting on my damn front porch while my son was in the yard playing basketball? I looked at TJ's ass like he had lost his everlasting mind.

"Drama, before you go off, give me a chance to explain what happened before you curse a nigga out," he said.

I invited them in because I wasn't about to show my ass in front of my son, and his ass knew that. I sent my son upstairs so that I could hear his dad speak his bullshit.

"Okay, I'm listening," I said.

"Listen, Drama, first let me say that this wasn't intentional. It just happened. You had me dropping our son over there for her to babysit on her days off, and we just started talking. Once I got to know her a little better, we started speaking on the phone and texting. Soon after, we started dating. Neither of us wanted to hurt you, but you and I are not together. I felt that we should at least come to you and tell you. That's the least I could do."

"Oh, so Hartley didn't tell you that she told a good friend of mine that she is pregnant by you before telling me?" I asked.

"No, she didn't tell me, but I'm sure she was just trying to get some feedback on the situation," he explained.

"What, the bitch can't speak? She had a lot to say when she was fucking you, right?"

"Drama, there's no need for the name calling."

I just disregarded him and got in Hartley's face.

"So you don't have anything to say? You come to my house pretending to be my fucking friend and my son's godmother, but your thirsty ass makes a move on my son's father?"

"Drama, I didn't know how to tell you—"

"So the bitch does speak!" I said, cutting her ass off. "First off, Hartley, nothing you can say to me can justify that you fucked my son's father, and if you're as sorry as you say, then why the fuck did I have to hear it from Trish? Tell me that, bitch!" I couldn't control my emotions any longer as I hauled off and slapped the bitch.

"Drama, she's pregnant! Have you lost your fucking mind?" TJ yelled.

"No, but clearly you did by bringing this bitch to my house and telling me this bullshit like shit is supposed to be sweet. Get this bitch out of my fucking house before she leaves in a body bag. And bitch, when you have that fucking baby, I'm fucking you up," I threatened.

That scary bitch didn't even wait for TJ. She bolted out the door.

When they were gone, I called Kindrah because I needed to vent. I couldn't believe this nigga had the audacity to bring this bitch to my house to tell me that she was pregnant and that they were a fucking couple. And then his dumb ass had the nerve to say that they didn't mean to hurt me? I meant just what I said: If I caught that bitch after she had that baby, I was fucking her up, and if TJ wanted to take up for her, he could get fucked up too.

KINDRAH

I had just gotten off the phone with Drama. She was upset, saying she couldn't believe that her baby's father came to the house with her friend, who he got pregnant. I thought that was big of him. I honestly can say that if Hartley hadn't run her mouth to Trish and had gone directly to Drama instead, she would have respected the situation more. I knew for a fact you never got over your first love, and even though it had been two years, I think Drama still loved TJ but would never admit it.

Amari finally came over with some soup and Dayquil. He didn't have the twins with him. They were with his father. It was a good thing he didn't. I didn't need my godbabies getting sick behind me because I wanted to fuck in the park.

"So how you feeling? Did the soup help any?" he asked.

"I feel a little better. I just hope this Dayquil helps me with my stuffy nose. I had some lemon and honey in my tea, so my throat feels a little better."

"What's up with you and Antwan? He didn't come to the twins' party, and now you're sick, and his ass isn't here. So what's going on?"

"He turned out to be a cheating asshole," I said. "At the rate I'm going, I'm starting to think that I will never be married with children. I just can't find a good man these days."

"You will. You just have to give it time. What's not to love about you? Some men just don't know a good thing when it's right in their face. Just take your time. I'm sure you will find Mr. Right," he said.

I wanted to say, "I found him, and he's sitting right in front of me."

Instead, I asked, "So what's up with you and Kelsey?"

"Who, Kells? We cool. I met her when I took one of my patients to Harlem Hospital for an appointment, and we been kicking it since that day."

I had to sit on my hands because I had this urge to choke the life out of his ass. The nerve of him. He knew I still loved his stank ass, so why did he still feel comfortable talking about a female to me? Okay, in the past when he didn't know how I felt about him and we had these discussions, I was cool with it because he didn't know that I was dying inside listening to him. But now, he was well aware of my feelings.

"Don't give me that look. You asked me a question, and I answered it. She did ask me if we ever had a relationship. She felt like you were giving her that ex-girlfriend stare-down." He laughed; I didn't.

"So what did you tell her?"

"I told her no because I didn't want to complicate anything if her and I were to become official. And being that we are best friends, I don't want her feeling uncomfortable," he said.

Really? Did he just say that to me? Amari better get up out of here before the twins grow up without a mom and a dad. His ass is really beginning to piss me off.

"Well, she doesn't have to worry about me if she's trying to pursue something with you. And make sure you tell her no need to ask any questions about me. And be sure to mention that if she has a problem with the friendship, she should remove herself now. I'm not going anywhere, and I'm not doing anything different to make her feel comfortable. That's your job," I said.

"She knows we are friends. I don't expect you to do anything differently, but it would be nice if you wouldn't be so rude. Trust, she knows we are best friends, and I will not choose her over you."

"I hope she does, because I don't have a problem telling her. And I wasn't trying to be rude. You didn't tell me you were seeing someone, so I was a little taken aback, that's all."

We sat talking for a little while longer, until it was time for him to go and pick up the girls. I told him once I was feeling better I would come and see the girls and spend some time with them.

SHELBY

I couldn't believe Dre's ass had done a 180. His freaky ass had not been requesting sex. This was a man who couldn't go without sex at all. He had to have it at least twice a day. So when we went from twice a day to no sex at all, my red flags went on alert. When I asked him what seemed to be the problem, he just said he'd been stressed with work. Bullshit. I knew his ass was fucking someone else, and he had better hope like hell I didn't find out who the bitch was.

"Dre, bring your ass upstairs," I yelled. "I'm horny. Your ass hasn't fucked me in a very long time, and I need some dick."

When he didn't answer, I took my ass downstairs. This nigga was laid out on the couch, sleeping. I was convinced now that something was up with his ass. I didn't give a fuck. Sleeping or not, this nigga was going to give me some dick. His ass looked all sexy laying there in his boxers.

I pulled out his semi-hard penis and started to stroke it until it was hard enough for me to ride. I positioned myself onto his stiff penis, put him inside of me, and started riding his shit, nice and slow. He woke up, and with no questions asked, he grabbed my hips and started working my ass just the way I liked. He flipped my big ass over the couch and fucked me doggy style. I really missed the dick.

"Oh my God, Dre." I came really fast once he hit my spot. It didn't take long for me, and he came right behind me, collapsing on my back.

It took him all of five minutes to be right back on my ass. Now, this was the Dre I'd been missing. I was sitting at the end of the couch, with my legs on his shoulders, as he ate my pussy like it was going to be his last meal. I grabbed his head and enjoyed the high I was on. I came at least two more times before his ass released me, and when I said I couldn't move, I mean I couldn't move. I had to lay in that position until I was able to get some strength in my legs to get up.

His ass hopped in the shower and was fully dressed by the time I was able to get up off of the couch.

"Where are you going, Dre? I thought you were spending the night," I said.

"Nah, I got to get up early tomorrow, and work is closer to my crib. If I stay here tonight, I will have to leave at like six a.m. just to make it in by eight."

I looked at his ass with hurt eyes. "Dre, who is she?"

"Don't start tripping. I just told you I had to get up early in the morning."

"Why the fuck are you lying? You went from fucking me every day and spending the night at least three times a week to not fucking me at all and not staying over. You expect me to believe you're not fucking nobody else?"

"I'm out. I just told your ass why I needed to leave, and you still here with the accusing bullshit. Call me later."

And with that, he walked out and slammed the door, waking up my son in the process. I knew that nigga was living foul. How the fuck was he just going to fuck me that good, get up, and bounce, treating me like a fucking booty call all of a sudden? Yeah, something was definitely up with his ass.

KINDRAH

Dre had the nerve to call and ask if his ass could still come and see me. Not happening. I had other plans, and it didn't involve his ass being between my legs. Not tonight anyway. I told him I would call him back.

I felt much better after taking medicine all day. I put on my black jeans, a black hoodie, and my black Tims. I grabbed my car keys and headed out.

I parked like three blocks away from where TJ lived. I opened my glove compartment, took out my black gloves and my .380, attaching the silencer. I loved having money. You could get your hands on just about anything. Don't ask me why I was at TJ's house. I couldn't explain why I felt the need to get at another lying-ass nigga.

I laid low in those damn bushes, and his ass never came home. I would catch his ass another time. I needed to find out where that bitch Hartley laid her head, because that was probably where his ass was laying his head that night.

I made sure to stop at the pharmacy to get some Thera-Flu. Hiding in those bushes had me feeling the same way I felt when my cold first started. I thought about calling Dre to come fuck me in the parking lot, but I quickly dismissed that idea. My ass was already sick as a dog. I needed to get home.

I really needed to stop acting crazy like this because this shit really wasn't making any sense to me. I think I was having some kind of chemical imbalance. How the hell could I be mad at Hartley when my ass was basically doing the same thing to Shelby? At least Drama and TJ weren't together anymore. Here I was fucking Dre when he and Shelby were clearly together and had been for years.

Anyway, no sense crying over what was done already, especially knowing I was not done fucking with him yet. As soon as he was done serving his purpose as being my much-needed distraction, I would be sending him back to Shelby. Like I said, Amari was my one and only love.

At home, I got in the bathtub and soaked my body, but not before I lit some vanilla-scented candles and poured a glass of Moscato. I just relaxed in the tub, thinking about Amari. I think all of this crazy behavior was because of him. I still loved him and wanted to be with him. He betrayed me like all the others, though, so I honestly didn't know what to do about this situation.

SHELBY

I got a babysitter so that Dre and I could go out one night. Lately we had been drifting apart, and I really had no idea why. I hadn't been doing anything different. All I did was go to work, come home, and care for my son. He insisted that he wasn't cheating on me, and it was the stress at work that had him so tired and distant. Yeah, right. Anyway, I was going to make the best out of our night to see if I could get my Dre back.

We ended up going to Neely's Barbecue Parlor on First Avenue. Once we were seated, we made small talk. I really didn't want to start an argument at the dinner table, but we had to have this discussion sooner or later.

"Babe, are you ready to tell me why you've been so distant? We went from not being able to be away from each other to not seeing each other at all. I love you, and I just want you to know that if it's something that I did, just let me know so that we can fix it," I said.

"Shell, you know I love you. A nigga has really just been stressed. My boss is on my ass every second of the day, even though all my contracts are up to par and the workers are getting the jobs done. He still insists on being a pain in the ass. You know a nigga loves you, and I would never distance myself on purpose. The truth is, I distance myself because I don't want to take my stress out on you when you are not the cause of it."

"Okay, babe, but you have to keep in mind that you can talk to me. You don't have to distance yourself. We're better than this."

"I know, Shell, and I promise I will do better because I'm not trying to lose my boo thang," he said.

We enjoyed our dinner and went home to fuck each other's brains out. When I got up to go to the bathroom, Dre's ass was knocked out. I wanted to believe that it was just work stressing him out, but my gut told a different story. I hoped that for once my gut was telling me wrong, but I knew that wouldn't be the case. My gut feeling was always right.

DRE

I really had to get my shit together. Kindrah had my nose wide open, and I'd been neglecting Shelby and her son, who had grown to love me as his father. The shit just wasn't right. I loved Shelby with my all. I didn't even know how a nigga had let a big butt and a smile knock me off my game. I was supposed to hit it and quit it like I did with all the others, but for some reason I couldn't get enough of her sweet pussy in my mouth or on my dick.

Damn, my shit got rock hard just thinking about it. A nigga had to get his mind right. I'd been trying to get at her for a few days now. I felt like a crack fiend trying to get my next hit, and the streets were dry. I promised myself that if she let me hit it one more time, I was done. I had to make shit right with me and my girl.

KINDRAH

Damn, Dre. Stop blowing up my fucking phone. Why can't his ass take a fucking hint? When I want dick, I will fucking answer his call. Leave me the fuck alone.

Again, he was the reason I felt the way I was feeling now. Nothing seemed to be working. I couldn't keep anything down, my head was killing me, and my throat was on fire. I had a doctor's appointment at 1 p.m., and Amari said he would take me.

We pulled up to Harlem Hospital Clinic at exactly 1 p.m. I went to sign in while Amari sat in the waiting area, texting on his phone. I bet his ass was talking to that bird bitch, Kelsey, since she worked over in the main hospital. That was probably why he offered to bring me to the clinic, so he could see her ass.

When I went over and sat next to him, he put his phone away.

"I hope you're not trying to hook up with your little friend while I'm sitting here sick," I said.

"Nah, I was just letting her know I was at the clinic with you, and she started tripping, asking me why I had to bring you to the doctor."

"And what did you say?"

"I told her to chill," he said.

"Whatever. I told you, sooner or later she's going to have an issue with our friendship."

"I already told her from the door that I refuse to let anyone come between our friendship or make me feel some kind of way about my friendship with you. I told her again that if she couldn't handle the friendship, to not even attempt to stay involved with me."

"Every girl you get involved with is going to be okay with it until they start catching feelings. So I guess Ms. Kelsey is feeling your yellow ass if she's starting to act up."

He didn't get a chance to answer because the nurse was calling me. When I got in the back, she took my vitals, and I told her the reason for my visit. I sat in the examination room, waiting for Dr. Sugupta.

"Hello, Ms. Watts. How are you feeling?"

"Not too good. My throat feels like it's on fire, and my nose is stuffy. None of the over the counter medicine is working."

She washed her hands and walked over to me. "Okay. Open up, and say ahhhh."

I laughed because I felt like a two-year-old.

By the time we were done, she told me that I had a sinus infection. She said I did have some redness of the throat, but that could have been caused by the coughing. She said that an antibiotic treatment wasn't needed but gave me a prescription for a decongestant.

I walked out and saw Kelsey sitting next to Amari, and I automatically caught an attitude. This bitch just had to come over there after he told the bitch he was with me.

"Amari, let's go!" I said with attitude.

"Why is she so fucking rude, Amari?" she asked.

"I told you she would have a problem with you coming over here, and you still came. Maybe she didn't want you to know she was at the doctor. I don't know her reason, but I asked you not to come over," Amari answered.

"So you're trying to tell me that you come to where I work, and just because you're here with your best friend, I'm not allowed to come and see you? Last time I checked, we were a couple, and that's what couples do. I wanted to see you, so I came over. If I knew she was going to make a big deal about it, I would have stayed my ass at my station."

"I'll holla at you later, Kells. Let me get out of here before she starts flipping," he said then followed me out the door.

KELSEY

Amari and Kindrah's friendship was really starting to get on my fucking nerves. He acted like she was his girl and not his fucking friend. Then she walked out like the queen bitch and didn't even speak. It was so fucking rude of her. I came over to say hello to his ass, and this bitch had the nerve to catch a fucking attitude. He didn't even check her ass but had the nerve to make excuses for her. I saw Kindrah and I were going to have big problems if she thought she was going to stand in the way of me being with Amari.

AMARI

Kindrah was pissed off with me. She didn't speak the whole ride back to her house, so I just drove in silence. I was hoping she calmed down by the time we got there.

I had no control of Kells walking over to the clinic, and Kindrah shouldn't have blamed me for it. She said she just wanted to be friends, but her actions were starting to say something else. I'd seen the jealousy a lot lately. If I looked at a female, her facial expressions changed. If we watched a movie and I made a comment about a female looking good, or even an innocent comment about the female's outfit, she caught an attitude.

My phone alerted me that I had a text message. I picked it up, read the text, and put my phone back in the cup holder. Kindrah shifted her body closer to the door like she was trying to control her emotions. I hoped that me dating again wasn't going to interfere with our friendship.

When I pulled up to her house, she got out and slammed the door. Usually I would go in after her, but I didn't feel like arguing, so I sat in the car for a few minutes to gather my thoughts and give her time to gather hers.

I texted Kells back while I waited for Kindrah to calm down. I didn't want to go inside and argue with Kindrah, but I was sitting in the car arguing with Kells. She wanted to know why I was still over at Kindrah's house. I just didn't understand how many times I had to tell this girl that Kindrah was my friend, and she was going to remain my friend. Kells was beginning to turn me off. She was starting to become clingy, and she tried to control my every move. To sum it all up, she was starting to act just how Tanisha used to act when it came to Kindrah, and I wasn't about to let anyone in my space if they even thought about hurting Kindrah.

KINDRAH

I sat watching Amari from the window, wondering if he was going to go or stay. I was hoping he stayed. I didn't mean to act like a spoiled brat, but I couldn't stand Kelsey. Something about her just didn't sit right with me, and I didn't trust her as far as I could throw her ass.

I went out to his car and knocked on his window. He lowered the window, and it looked like he was in the middle of a heated conversation. I guess he got tired of texting the bitch, so he called her. Once the window was down, I told him I forgot to get my prescription from the pharmacy. He told me to give it to him, and he would run and get it.

"Bring back something to eat," I said and smiled, letting him know we were good.

I went back into the house, stripped out of my clothes, and took a relaxing shower. Afterward, I put on a tank and some boy shorts and went to my computer to check my e-mail. My realtor had some postings of houses that she wanted me to look at, and if I liked any, she wanted me to give her a call so she could make the appointments to see the properties.

By the time I was done, Amari was in the kitchen putting the food on plates. He had picked up Chinese takeout. I didn't feel like sitting at the table, so I went to eat in the living room. I thought he was going to get me some real food, but I was wrong. He got me some chicken noodle soup. I didn't want that shit! Yeah, my throat hurt, but my ass was hungry, and this soup wasn't going to fill me up.

I put the movie *Something Borrowed* into the DVD player. I loved this movie. It kind of reminded me of me and Amari. He turned up his nose to my selection, but I didn't care; he was going to watch it.

After I finished my soup, he got my medicine so I could take the first dose. Hopefully it would give me some relief for my throat. I wanted to kiss him so bad. Even if he would let me, I knew that I couldn't since I was sick.

I was getting sleepy. The medication made me a little drowsy, and because Amari didn't have to work that night, he stayed with me. He agreed to go with me in the morning to see a couple of the places that my realtor called and said were available to view.

We slept in the same bed that night, and it took everything in me not to seduce him, sick and all. My hormones were screaming for that feeling he used to give me between my legs. I put my thoughts to bed as I drifted off to a much-needed sleep.

AMARI

When Kindrah came out to the car, I was on the phone with Kells, and she heard Kindrah tell me that she forgot her medication. So when I told her I would pick it up for her, Kelsey lost it. She started accusing me of fucking Kindrah and threatening me, talking about if I stayed there I didn't have to ever worry about her calling me again. I had to hang up the phone on her because she was really making me want to curse her ass out and tell her to stop being so damn insecure.

She had been ringing my phone and texting me nonstop, and I had to turn my phone off. It was something that I hated to do, because my dad had the twins with him, but I would just have to keep checking on them.

When I got back to Kindrah's, she was so hyped when she saw the Chinese food, until she saw that I got her ass some chicken noodle soup. She didn't like that at all, but how was she going to eat her favorite chicken lo mein with chicken wings if her throat was still hurting her?

We sat up in the living room and watched some corny-ass love movie that she wanted to watch. I really enjoyed being in her space, and I really did wish that what we could have worked out. Sometimes it was hard being around her and not being able to touch her like I used to. When we used to be just friends, before we started having a sexual relationship, we cuddled all the time. To do it now wouldn't be comfortable because it would definitely turn sexual.

After she took her medication, she was getting sleepy, so I told her I would stay the night with her. We put the television on in the bedroom and got into her bed, her on her side and me on mine, and we watched another movie until we both drifted off to sleep.

I was up before Kindrah, so I went to the guest room to pick out an outfit for the day. Yes, I had clothes in her guest room. After I showered, I went to the kitchen. I made Kindrah some oatmeal and a cup of lemon and honey tea, and then made me a breakfast fit for a king.

"Oh, hell no. How I get some damn oatmeal and you get all of that?" she complained.

"Do we have to have the same conversation from last night? Aren't you sick? Once you feel better, I will come back and make you a breakfast fit for a queen."

"Whatever, Amari. Anyway, how long have you been up?"

"I've been up for a while. I got up to check on the girls and to see if my father will keep them while I go with you to look at a couple of places. And not to mention, when I turned my phone back on this morning, I had so many texts and phone messages from Kells. I'm starting to think that she is going to be on some stalker type shit. I can understand that she's not feeling our friendship, but I didn't keep our friendship a secret. She said she was okay with it, but being that you were acting all jealous and shit, she now doesn't believe that we are only friends."

"Whatever. Don't blame me because you always end up with them crazy hoes. But what I will say is, if she's acting as if she's going to be a problem, let her walk now because you don't need to have that type of behavior around my godbabies."

"Yeah, after we get back later, I'm going to pick up my girls, go home, call her, and let her know that this isn't going to work. I'm looking for someone who can handle my relationship with you. Someone who knows how to separate the two, meaning my love for you takes nothing away from them."

"Yeah, whatever. You better not love anyone more than you love me, and you can stop trying to fill that void you're feeling. There's no one out there who's going to give you that loving feeling," she said, smiling.

"Whatever. Finish eating and take your medication so we can get going."

Once I left Kindrah's and picked the twins up from my dad, I decided to go home and spend some time with them. That was short lived. I pulled up to my place, and Kells was parked in my driveway, wearing a mean mug. I gave her a look that warned her not to show her ass in front of my girls.

"I just came by because you refused to respond to any of my calls or my text messages," she said.

It felt like I was about to have to deal with the crazy again, and I really didn't have the patience. I had enough of crazy. What was up with women these days?

"Let me put the twins down for a nap, and then we can talk."

"Okay, fine. I will be in the living room waiting on you," she said.

Did she just invite herself in?

I wasn't trying to be rude, but I really didn't want her inside. Instead of putting up a fight, I told her to make herself comfortable. I went to the kitchen and fixed the twins' bottles. I carried them up to their room, putting each of them down for a nap. It didn't take long to get them down. I have good babies.

I walked downstairs to see Kells snooping around. When I had said to make herself comfortable, I didn't mean walk around looking at shit. I meant sit her ass down. She sat down on the couch once she realized I was in the room.

"Okay, so what do you want to talk about?" I asked.

"I just want to know why you got mad at me and ignored my calls because I questioned you about Kindrah. If nothing is going on with you two, why was it such a big problem to ask why you were still at her house? And then to hear her ask you to bring something back to eat only meant you were leaving and coming back to her house. If we are just starting out and trying to get to know each other, how is that supposed to happen if you're always spending time with Kindrah?"

"Kells, when we first got together, you were told that Kindrah was my best friend and there would be times when it would look as if we are in a relationship, because that's how close we are. I also told you if you couldn't handle me having that kind of friendship with her, then there would be no reason for us to pursue this. You told me you weren't insecure, and you could respect my friendship with Kindrah."

"That's true, but I didn't know she was going to be rude and acting like a jealous girlfriend. I've done nothing but be pleasant to her. Nothing less, nothing more. And instead of you getting all bent out of shape because I asked a question, you should have been checking her ass and letting her know she should show me the same respect that I showed her."

"I told you that Kindrah has trust issues when it comes to females. Before you came over, she asked me not to have you come to the clinic because she is very private when it comes to her business. I apologize for even telling you that she had an appointment at the clinic. I also told her you weren't going to come over, so for her to come out and see you sitting there made her upset—not at you, but me.

"I got upset because I told you I would see you later, and you still showed up like you were trying to prove something, and I don't have time for that shit because there is no competition when it comes to Kindrah. She is a part of my life, and she's going to always be a part of my life. Based on how you acted today, and we've only been seeing each other for a few months, I don't think this is going to work," I told her.

"Are you serious? How do you figure this isn't going to work? After one argument you're calling it quits?" she asked.

"Had you been around long enough, I would have told you the history of me and Kindrah, and once you knew what we've been through, you would have had a better understanding. You couldn't even respect the fact that I have a female friend with trust issues. And I promised you that once she got to know you, she would have opened up to you, but you fucked that up. So no, I can't continue to have a relationship with you because I can't have you causing problems in my friendship."

"Wow, you're really serious. Un-fucking believable. Now, if I did believe you two were only friends, I damn sure don't believe it now. Who breaks off a relationship because your girl doesn't get along with your female friend? That's unheard of."

"Okay, you're missing the fucking point, and I'm tired of arguing about it because you just don't get it. You were disrespectful by leaving all of those phone calls and text messages and threats. I don't care if you were upset. All that was uncalled for. I told you I don't do drama, especially around my children. If you have nothing else to say, I would like for you to leave," I said.

She got up to leave and slammed my door so hard that I thought she was going to break the window. I felt bad, but all that shit she said really was crazy. Having a phone tantrum was not a good look.

SHELBY

Everything had been going good between me and Dre. He was back to being himself. We even decided to stop paying double bills and move in with each other. He wanted me to give up my condo, but I told him hell no. He lived in the hood, and I wasn't about to have my son around that madness. It took some convincing, but he agreed, so we were in the process of making the transition.

We were at his place packing boxes and throwing some things out. He really didn't have too much stuff to pack because he had a bachelor's pad. The only things he was keeping were his clothes. His furniture, televisions, and kitchen stuff was all being distributed amongst his family members.

Dre was upstairs putting his clothes into the boxes, and I was downstairs in the kitchen putting all of his dishes and pots and pans into boxes. His phone was on the counter and it kept going off, alerting him that he had a text message. I ignored the first three alerts, but curiosity was getting the best of me. I never entertained the idea of snooping on Dre, but because of his actions a few weeks ago, my trust alert was on high.

Against my better judgment, I picked up the phone, and almost immediately, the pain in my heart hit me full force. My hands began to shake, and I felt sick to my stomach. The tears just wouldn't stop. I heard Dre walk into the kitchen. He looked concerned, until he saw his phone in my hand. His face went from concerned to guilty.

"Why, Dre? Why? I asked you if you were seeing someone else, and I asked you to be honest with me."

"What are you talking about?" he stuttered.

I watched as he took the phone from my hand and began reading the text messages.

"Shell, this bitch is crazy, and she's lying. She has been texting and calling me since the day of the party, trying to get at me."

"So I look fucking stupid to you? How did she get your fucking number? Last I checked, I knew how to fucking read. The bitch said she's ready for some more of that good dick, nigga. She didn't text when can she get some dick."

"Shell, listen, I'm sorry. It was one time, and I was going to tell you. Please, just listen to me."

"Dre, don't fucking touch me. That's why the bitch stopped calling me, and now I suppose the real reason she didn't invite me and Jamel to her godchildren's birthday party was because she was fucking your ass. It makes perfect sense now."

"Come on, Shell. I made a mistake. You know how much I love you. I got caught up, but I'm back, baby. You don't have to ever worry about me fucking with her again. I'm sorry, babe. Please don't leave me," he said.

"Don't fucking leave you? Nigga, you fucked one of my friends. Why wouldn't I leave your sorry ass? I have always been faithful to you. I fucked you every time you wanted to fuck, cooked for you, and would do anything for you because that's what love is. But I guess you didn't get the fucking memo. If your ass was going to fuck around, why did you have to fuck someone in my circle? Why not a random bitch? Then this bitch is going to stop fucking with me like I did something wrong." I got so mad, I started throwing shit all over the place. I wanted to grab a fucking knife and cut his fucking dick off, but my son's face popped in my head, and common sense started to kick in.

"Fuck you, Dre, and fuck this relationship. I'm done, so you can go and give the bitch what she's asking for because you will never touch me again. Ever."

I pulled out of his driveway and made it about two blocks before I had to pull over. The tears wouldn't stop. I wanted to hurt him the way he hurt me, but I wanted to hurt Kindrah even more. Why would she do this to me? I befriended her, even when Kimora and Drama didn't want her to be a part of our circle because something about her just wasn't right. We decided to let the psycho in anyway.

I tried to get my breathing back to normal before I got back on the road. It would be just my luck to get in a fucking car crash, even though the way my heart was broken, it might not have even have mattered except for my son. I lived for Jamel, and I'd be damned if I didn't make it back home to my baby.

I ended up going straight to Drama's house because I was a mess, and I knew that Dre would eventually show up to my house. I wasn't in the mood to listen to his ass talk about how sorry he was.

"Girl, what are you doing here? Why you crying? What happened? Shell, talk to me. What's going on?" Drama asked.

I couldn't even speak as I watched her call Kimora downstairs.

"Who the fuck I got to fuck up? Tell me what's going on right now, Shelby."

"We let that bitch Kindrah in our circle, and I found out she's been fucking Dre. I was at his house helping his ass pack his shit to move in with me, and his phone kept going off. I was going to ignore it, but it just kept alerting him of a text message. Now, you know I have never checked his phone or even thought about going through any of his things, but being he was missing in action and we'd stopped having sex, I've been having red flags, so my curiosity got the best of me. It was this bitch asking him when she could get the dick again."

"Are you sure it was Kindrah? I'm in shock. How the fuck did she sit in my face and have a problem with what Hartley was doing, and the bitch turned around and did the same bullshit?" Drama asked.

"Don't beat yourself up about it. You had no way of knowing that bitch was going to go after Dre. Did you try calling her ass to see what the fuck she had to say about this foul shit?" Kimora asked.

"No, I didn't call her, and I didn't go by her house because I'm really afraid of what I might do to this bitch."

KINDRAH

Dre had the nerve to call me and tell me that Shelby found out about us. I had to tell that nigga that there was no us. We fucked, and that was the extent of it. I just hoped a bitch didn't get beside herself and try and step to me, because she was really going to regret the day she met me.

I knew Drama and Kimora were riding with her, but I couldn't give two shits about it. I was just glad I didn't get the chance to eliminate Drama's baby's father because that bitch should have gotten played. She was a weak bitch, and Kimora's ass was, too. I wished she would even think about stepping to me. She told me too much of her business to fuck with me. I would have the feds kicking in her motherfucking boyfriend's door by the morning.

I guess I was back to not having any friends, and did I care? Hell no. As long as I had Amari, that was all that mattered. He told me he gave Kelsey the boot, so it was just me, him, and the twins, just the way I liked it. I just had to let him know that I still loved him and wanted to try at a relationship again, because the twins needed a mother figure in their life. Who better to take that place than their godmother?

Since I had bitches gunning for my head, I decided to call my realtor and tell her that I wanted the place that she had showed me the other day. I asked her how soon before I could move in. She confirmed that as soon as I gave her the first month's rent and security deposit, I could move in.

Originally, I was going to purchase a home, but I changed my mind. If things worked in my favor, I would be moving in with Amari, so renting was a better option for right now. I called Amari to let him know that I took the first place that we had looked at the other day, and he was happy, claiming that he would help me move and get settled in.

I was leaving the realtor's office and decided to go get some lunch. I ran into Robin and a few other people from the job. We hugged and she said how much she missed me. I decided to sit and have lunch with them.

"It's been so long, Kindrah. You don't even call me anymore. I tried calling you a few times to let you know that Antwan hasn't returned to work, and a missing person's report has been filed. Have you spoken to him?"

"No, I haven't spoken to him since the day you told me he was dating Monique."

"Well, she hasn't heard from him either. She's the one who filed the missing person's report. She took a leave from work because she is really distraught behind his disappearance, and she just found out she was pregnant a few weeks ago."

"Oh, wow. Like I said, I was so upset with him that I didn't even reach out to him anymore. I was hurt and didn't want anything to do with him, but I hope that he is found okay because I wouldn't wish anything bad on him." I pretended like I was upset and excused myself. I told Robin I would call her soon, and if she heard anything about Antwan to let me know. I had to get out of there because I was tempted to say "fuck that nigga." I truly didn't give a shit that his ass was missing.

Can you believe Dre was hitting me up, asking me if we could meet somewhere to talk? Against my better judgment, I agreed to meet up with him because I had dick on the brain. When he asked me to meet him at Flushing Meadow Park, I didn't think anything of it because he had this fetish of fucking in the park.

I got to the park about twenty minutes later, but I didn't see his truck, so I parked and waited. Out of nowhere, my door opened and I was being dragged out of the car. I tried to fight off whoever had grabbed me, but there were a few of them. All I could do was try my best to protect my face. The kicking finally stopped, and that's when I heard her voice. It was Shelby.

"So you like fucking with other women's men?" she yelled as she kicked me in my back. "Get up, bitch, so I can kick your fucking ass the way you deserve it."

I tried to get up, but the pain in my stomach was too much. She started kicking me again. I heard Kimora telling her to stop, but she kept kicking.

"Fuck that bitch, Kimora. We let her in our circle, and this is what the bitch does? She goes and fucks one of our fucking men!" screamed Drama. "Let's just go before someone calls the cops."

Shelby spit in my face and told me if she saw me again, she was going to kick my ass again, and I better stay away from Dre.

She would definitely be seeing me again. *All those bitches,* I thought as she kicked me one last time. Everything went black.

Someone called the authorities, but by the time they arrived, those bitches were gone already. When they got there, I was awake and trying to get up but couldn't.

I was taken to the emergency room, even though I tried to refuse. The EMT said that I should go to make sure I didn't have any internal bleeding. I was questioned by the police, but I didn't tell them anything about Shelby being my attacker. I just told them that someone was trying to take my Range Rover.

Amari came to the hospital. I didn't tell him the truth either. I just told him that someone tried to carjack me, and when I refused, they pulled me out of the car and started assaulting me. Basically the same story I told the police, but I told him that before they could take my truck, a couple of bystanders scared them off.

I decided that I wouldn't go after them just yet. I wanted them to think that I wasn't going to retaliate, but you best believe they would be seeing me.

I had to stay at the hospital overnight but was released the next morning. Amari drove me to pick my truck up from the police parking lot. They were nice enough to have it towed to their lot. Once we got my car, he followed me back to my place. We decided we would start packing my things to be moved over to my new place in Queens Village, not too far from his place. Amari did most of the work because my body was still sore.

When I went to take a shower, I wanted to cry looking at all the black and blue marks all over my body. I decided to skip the shower and soaked my body in a tub of hot water.

Amari was almost done by the time I got out of the tub. It was so relaxing that I almost fell asleep until he knocked on the door. He stayed until it was time for him to go to work. After he left, I went to my room to watch a movie.

I got a call from Dre, apologizing. He said he had no idea that Shelby used his phone to set me up. He said he only found out what she did after he overheard them speaking about it. I believed him, so when he asked if he could come over, I told him yes. Shit, by the end of the week, this would no longer be my place of residence, so I didn't mind him coming over and fucking my brains out. The stupid bitch attacked me, and it didn't keep her man from coming to serve me the dick again. If I wasn't in love with Amari, I would have made him my man. That would have been the ultimate payback.

Dre was ringing my bell. I was a little leery that it may have been another setup, so I put my gun in the pocket of my robe. When I opened the door, it was just his sexy ass. I let him in and locked the door.

As soon as he saw my face, he kept apologizing. I told him not to worry about it. I didn't want to talk about it; I just wanted to be fucked. I let him know that he had to be gentle because my body was killing me.

This would be the first time we actually had sex indoors. We went up to the bedroom. He kissed my body from head to toe. When he reached my honey pot and sucked all my honey up, I was ready for the dick. He entered me, and I felt like I was in heaven. Because I was in so much pain, he was taking his time with me, but I wanted to fuck. I became the aggressor and told him to fuck me doggy style, my favorite position. He beat it up so good that I collapsed with him on my back. Once he moved, I crawled to the top of the bed, and he laid his head in my lap and held me around my waist. If I wasn't already in love with someone, he could definitely be that dude.

Once he fell asleep, I picked up my phone and sent Shelby a text.

Kindrah: So you and your sidekicks felt the need to kick my ass over a nigga that clearly likes this pussy better than yours.

Shelby: Sure you right, bitch. He fucked you because just like any other man, they get a thrill out of fucking hoes. Trust and believe he will never fuck your stink-ass pussy again. He knows where home is.

I knew she wouldn't believe me, so the next text I sent was a picture message of her man, lying between my legs. No response.

Thirty minutes into a good sleep, this bitch was banging on my fucking door. I woke Dre up to tell him that Shelby was at the door. He looked like a scared little bitch.

I guess we were taking too long to come to the door, and this bitch must've started hitting a car because the alarm was blaring. I heard glass breaking, and I was praying that this bitch wasn't fucking with my ride.

Dre saw the look in my eyes, and when he saw me grab my gun and head downstairs, he had the nerve to say, "Chill. I got this."

I heard the two dummies going back and forth in my yard, so I went to the door and pointed my gun at both of them. I told them they had ten seconds to get from in front of my house, and she better be glad it was his ride and not mine. The bitch wasn't stupid. She didn't have anything to say.

I closed my door and locked it. Payback felt good. A bitch was always so fast to jump on the next bitch, but forgave the no-good nigga that played her stupid ass. She called herself fucking me up and taking him back, just to catch him with his drawers down. Again. I could have killed the bitch, but she wasn't worth it, and neither was he. I went back upstairs, got in my bed, and slept like a baby.

The movers were at my place by 11 a.m. the next morning. I had my next door neighbor looking at me sideways. I didn't care. His ass was probably in the window watching the show last night, and he was probably happy to see me moving out. There had been plenty of times I had to curse his ass out about his annoying-ass dog that I had to kill because as long as that dog was breathing, I couldn't ever get a good night's sleep. His old ass had the nerve to put up flyers asking for help to locate that pain in the ass.

I followed the movers to my new place. Once they were done unloading, I headed back over to my old place.

I was knocking those bitches down one by one. Kimora's boyfriend's place got raided the night before, and it was all over the news. Drama was out on administrative leave without pay, thanks to yours truly. I called up to her job, pretending to be a parent of one of the patients that she told me she basically abused every chance she got. *Stupid bitch. Now see how you pay your fucking bills.*

Once I got back to the old place, I did a walk-through to make sure I didn't forget anything. I was too happy to be moving out. My new place was a gated community, so if anyone found out where I laid my head, they would have to be announced, so I felt better about that. I had enemies now, and I refused to get caught slipping again.

TANISHA

I didn't know how much more I could take of this place. From the first day I got to the freak show of a facility, they had been medicating me and trying to get me to talk. And now that I was talking, no one was listening to what I had to say. It just didn't make any sense to me, but I was the crazy one.

I had to get in touch with Amari. It was going to be hard trying to convince him to come and just hear me out. I was facing so many charges, and for once in my life, I could honestly say that I was scared. My lawyer said we could plead insanity, and I told his ass I wasn't taking a plea. The hospital had me scheduled to talk to a psychologist twice a week, but after he refused to write down what I was trying to tell him about my case and what information I had for the authorities, I refused to speak to him at all. Now my visits were spent just looking at his white ass for the whole hour, saying nothing.

I knew he had already made up in his mind as to what he wanted to believe about me. The one thing that I could say was that the medication was working because all I did was think about my babies and Amari and how I wished that we could go back to being a family. I now understand why Amari gave up on me: I had given up on myself.

I started a new journal that I wrote in every day, and this one was asking for forgiveness for all that I had done. After my session one day, I wrote Amari a letter asking him if he could find it in his heart to come and visit me. I needed to speak with him. I knew that somewhere in his heart he still cared for me, because in the report my lawyer read to me, there was no mention about a gun.

I cried myself to sleep every night being in that place. I couldn't imagine being locked up for the rest of my life and not seeing my babies, and I was praying that they didn't get this disorder. I asked the doctor about it, and he told me that bipolar disorder often ran in families. There was a genetic part to this mood disorder, so to say that I was praying for them would be an understatement.

AMARI

I received a letter from Tanisha. She told me that her treatment was going well and asked me how the twins were doing. She said she wished that she could make things how they were before, and she said she didn't want to discuss too much in the letter. She also asked if I could visit her. I'm not going to sit here and lie; I honestly forgave her. She had a sickness, and she lost control.

She wanted me to come the next weekend, but I couldn't make that visit. I would try for the following weekend when my dad was off, so that he could keep the twins with him. I would ask Kindrah if she could come with me for support. I sat and wrote Tanisha a letter back, letting her know that I would be there the following weekend.

It was beginning to look like I was going to have to change my phone number, because Kelsey had been calling and texting me on some stalker shit. When I left work the other night, I could have sworn I saw her car parked across the street from the facility. The twins were scheduled for a doctor's appointment the next day, so we were spending the night at Kindrah's new place. She was accompanying me to the appointment because the last time I took them to get shots, I couldn't handle both of them. They went off, and it took me, the nurse, and the doctor to hold them down. I thought Tiara would be the good one, but I was wrong. I knew once she started, Tania was going to follow suit.

My babies were getting so big, and I felt kind of bad that they were growing up without their mother. Kindrah had been a lifesaver and they loved her to death, but Tanisha was their mother. Hopefully, they would be able to visit her once I knew for sure the medication was working and she was in her right state of mind.

After the twins woke up from their naps, I fixed them something to eat. While they ate in their highchairs, I started to get the overnight bags ready. I made sure I had their shot records and the insurance cards for the appointment the next day. I packed a few jars of food and juice. I couldn't forget the sippy cups because they would have a fit if I didn't have them.

We got to Kindrah's new place, and I was really feeling the new setup. The guard was already familiar with me, so he opened the gate and I drove right in. Kindrah was standing on the porch, waiting for me pull up. She came over to the car to help me with the twins.

I'd been feeling a little anxious all day because I wanted to have a very important conversation with her. We played with the twins until it was time for them to have dinner, get baths, and be put to bed. Kindrah made dinner for the two of us, and we sat at the dining room table to eat. I was picking at my food because I was nervous, and when I started biting my bottom lip, Kindrah knew something was up. When she asked me what was wrong, I took a deep breath and took her hands into mine.

"Okay, I have been thinking about this for some time now. I want to know how you feel about us being together again as a couple. I never stopped loving you, and after the fallout with Kelsey, I came to realize that it didn't matter who I started seeing. It would be the same situation over and over—me not being able to give them my all because I'm very much still in love with you. I know I put you through a lot the first time we tried to be together, but I promise you that I'm all in this time. I don't want to be with anyone but you—if you'll still have me. I know that you have trust issues, and I want you to know that I never lied to you on purpose. It was always to protect your feelings.

"The girls love you just as much as I love you, and I would love for us to live together as a family. I'm not asking you to come in and take Tanisha's place as their mother, because she will always be their mother.

"I also need to know if you do agree to give us another chance, will you be able to accept Tanisha being a part of their life? I don't know what her fate is right now, but she wrote me a letter asking me if I could come and visit her. I told her that I couldn't come next week, but I will be making the trip the following week, and I would like for you to make that trip with me. She said the medication is working for her, and she is doing fine. So if this visit goes okay and I see that she is in a good state of mind, I would like to start taking the girls to visit her at least once a month. So how do you feel about everything that I just said?"

Kindrah started tearing up. I walked over and kneeled down in front of her, wiping her tears.

"Amari, I would love to start a relationship with you. I never stopped loving you, and I think you knew that all along. Being with you is all I've ever wanted, and you know I love the girls just like they were mine. I will never try to replace their mother, but I will love them all the same.

"Yes, I have trust issues because the last time I gave you my heart, you broke it into a million pieces. If we are going to do this again, I need you to be honest with me about any and everything. For starters, I want you to tell me why you kept the knowledge from me that Tanisha was the person who caused my accident. You could have told me. It wasn't like you knew in the beginning that she did that to me; you had no way of knowing. I'm sure when you found out, you were shocked, but that's something you should have shared with me.

"And as far as the girls being a part of Tanisha's life, I would never have a problem with that, as long as they are safe. I would never want to keep them away from their mom."

"Kindrah, listen. When I found out that she was responsible for your accident, I was shocked, and I was hurt at the same time. I didn't understand why she would do something like that to you, but once it was brought to my attention that she was dealing with mental issues, I realized that it was her disorder that played a very big part in hurting you. When the police came to my door and told me something that I already knew, I didn't tell them of her whereabouts because her parents told me that she was getting the help that she needed. I didn't feel the need to have her put in jail because she would have gotten lost in the system and never received the help she needed. Now I'm sorry that I kept that from you, and I hope that you can forgive me, and we can move on."

"Amari, I say yes to us being a couple again, but I just need for you to give me a couple of weeks. I have some things to figure out. Things I don't want to bring into the relationship. So if you can agree to that, then I'm in."

I stood her up, kissed her, and gave her a big hug. I told her I would wait a lifetime for her.

KINDRAH

I tried to be happy about Amari and me being a couple again, but I had to put that to the side. Once we finished making love last night, I sat up in the dark thinking about the letter he said he got from Tanisha. I just got him back in my life, and I wasn't going to let anything or anyone come between us again. I now understand why he kept what Tanisha did to me a secret. He loved me and was trying to protect me; but he had also been in love with Tanisha at one time or another, and he felt the need to protect her as well. I got it now, and I forgave him, but would he be as forgiving if he found out what I'd done? I wasn't sure, but what I was sure of was not taking that chance. I had less than a week to do what needed to be done.

We arrived at the doctor's office, and it was like the twins remembered the last time they were there, because they were crying and being really cranky. I rocked Tania in my arms, trying to comfort her. After a while, she finally quieted down. Amari had Tiara sleeping.

The visit went well, and he dropped me off to my place. He left to go home, and I told him I would call him later on that night before I went to bed. I think he could tell I had something on my mind. I just hoped he didn't think I was having second thoughts.

I booked a flight to Georgia. The earliest flight I could get was leaving on Friday morning. When I spoke to Amari, I told him that I was going to Atlantic City with the girls for Drama's birthday, and he actually believed me. He didn't have a reason not to. He didn't know that I'd had a falling out with them because I slept with Dre, so that worked out just fine.

I arrived in Georgia and was really nervous about pulling this off. It was going to be hard, but I had to do what needed to be done. My first stop was to a residence where I paid good money to pick up my fake ID. Next, I went and purchased a blond wig and hazel contacts, just like the female was wearing in the photo on the ID. I must say it was a perfect match. No questions should be asked about the ID. I just had to remember that my name was Tyjanae Williams. Yes, ghetto as hell, but I wasn't trying to raise any red flags. If anyone was trying to locate me after the fact, how many women named Tyjanae do you know?

I lied and told the facility that I was Tanisha's cousin, so they were expecting me.

Everything went well as far as getting into the facility, and because Tanisha had made progress, she was no longer confined nor needed supervised visits. The visiting room was set up like a living room area. I sat on one of the couches, waiting for someone to bring her down. When she walked in the room, she was hesitant because I didn't look like myself.

"Are you sure you're visiting the right person? I think there has been some kind of mistake," she said.

"There has been no mistake. I'm visiting the right person, Tanisha."

"Kindrah," she said in a low voice with a look of shock on her face.

"Yes, it's me. I bet you never expected to see me again. Have a seat, and if you do anything to alert anyone, I'm going to make sure your precious twins don't see their second birthday."

She sat down, and I got down to the reason I was there. "I know you have questions, but let me give you a little history on why I had to kill your parents. When the officers came to see me and told me that you were the person responsible for my accident, they said that they had gotten your last known address from your DMV records. I wasn't even really upset because you have always been jealous of me, but when they told me that Amari told them he didn't know of your whereabouts, I was hurt.

"So they didn't give up on trying to locate you. Officer Creer told me that you listed a Tammy and Gerald Watkins as your next of kin at your place of employment. When they mentioned your parents' names and stated they were from Georgia, I stood there in shock. I told the officers to keep me posted.

"See, the mention of those names clicked, because those were the names of my biological parents, who gave me up to the Watts family and moved to Georgia.

"My adopted siblings are who always made sure to remind me that I was adopted. My seventeen-year-old adopted brother showed me my original birth certificate at the tender age of twelve because I didn't believe him. Why they still had my original birth certificate, I have no idea. They teased me every day and made sure to make me feel like an outcast. By the time I turned fourteen, I hated all of them for lying to me and treating me bad.

"I never let my adoptive parents know that I knew I was adopted because Stephen told me he would kill me if I told his parents he was the one who told me I was adopted. A few weeks later, my adopted mother told me that I could go to my best friend's birthday sleepover, and I was excited to get away from them, even if it was only for a night.

"My joy was short lived because my adopted brother told his mom that my teacher called and said that I was disobedient and had to be sent to the principal's office. He also told her that they needed her to come in on Monday morning. I tried to tell her that he was lying, but being it was Friday and after school hours, there was no way for me to prove it to her. She had no reason not to believe her son, because she never knew of the hatred the siblings had toward me or all of the mistreatment that took place in her home. She told me that I couldn't go to the sleepover. I ran to my room and cried like a baby. I didn't talk to anyone, and I refused to eat dinner.

"That night, when everyone was sleeping, I grabbed my sleeping bag and backpack, and I set them on the back porch. I went back inside and removed all the batteries from the smoke detectors. I started in the living room, lighting the curtains on fire, and did the same in the dining room. Once in the kitchen, I turned on all of the burners on the stove and left out the back door, locking it behind me. I ran the two blocks to my best friend's sleepover," I said, finishing my story.

"So you're trying to say my parents were your parents, and you killed them for giving you up? I don't believe you." Tanisha was in shock.

"Well, it doesn't matter if you believe me or not, but I do know I'm just as crazy as you. So it has to be some truth to what I'm saying, don't you think?"

"If you killed your parents, who you say were your adopted parents, how come every year on the anniversary of their death you were always visiting their graves? It just doesn't make sense," she said.

"It makes perfect sense. How could I not visit my parents' and siblings' graves, who I loved so much? I would love to stay and entertain you a little longer, but I have to get home to my boyfriend and my daughters. I'll be sure to give them a kiss for you." I started laughing a crazy laugh that I had no control of. It was like my sanity had left the building.

She got up and rushed me. She had me on the floor and began banging my head on the floor. Just as I was losing consciousness, the staff came rushing in. They grabbed Tanisha and escorted her out of the room. She continued to fight them, and they had to give her something to calm her down. I told the safety officers that she attacked me for no reason, and I told them that all I did was ask her about how her treatment was going.

Because she was there for murder, and not to mention she was bipolar, they believed me and I was free to go. What they didn't know was that Tanisha would be dead by morning.

The same guy that I had paid to get me the fake ID to get into the mental hospital had a cousin who was as shady as they came. It just so happened that she was a nurse that worked at the facility on the unit where Tanisha was being treated. She agreed to inject Tanisha with some drug that would stop her breathing. She said that the drug wouldn't be able to be traced, so she was supposed to make it look like a suicide by cutting her wrists once she stopped breathing.

Tanisha's whole family were Jehovah's Witnesses, and they didn't believe in having an autopsy performed. Their beliefs were that the dead were conscious of nothing, but the body was created by Jehovah God and should not be mutilated. So I had no worries.

I paid the nurse five thousand dollars up front, and when I was sure she did the job, she would get the other five thousand.

Too bad she wouldn't get the pleasure of spending any of the money. She would meet the same fate that her cousin had met as soon as he gave me the fake ID. One thing I learned was to never leave witnesses and always cover your tracks. That was exactly what I planned to do, and then I would be on my plane back home by Sunday night.

When I got back to New York, I went straight home, took a long shower, and called Amari to let him know that I was back in town. When his father picked up his phone, I knew something was wrong. His father informed me that Tanisha had passed away that morning. I gasped and told him that I was on my way. I grabbed my keys and left right back out. Even though I was tired as hell, I had to play my part.

When I got to Amari's, he was sitting on the couch with his face in his hands. I went over and rubbed his back in a comforting manner, but I was pissed the fuck off inside that his ass was so upset about her death. I played it off. I decided to just be there. I guessed when he was ready to talk, he would talk.

I took care of the twins, giving them a bath, putting them in their beds with a bottle, and turning on the nightlight as I closed the door. Amari's dad was in the guest bedroom, and I went in to see if he was okay. He said he was fine and said that Tanisha's body was going to be flown there. He was going to make all of the arrangements for her going home ceremony.

Amari took Tanisha's death harder than I thought he would. He began blaming himself, and for some reason he felt that if he had gone to see her when she asked, she would still be alive. He was starting to really get on my damn nerves. She was dead and gone. He needed to get over it already.

Tanisha's death was ruled a suicide, and I made sure the dumb, greedy nurse gave me Tanisha's journal and a few of her other personal items. I made sure to burn them. I thought I was going to feel some type of way because we were blood sisters, but I didn't. She grew up with parents who loved her, and I grew up being mistreated by my siblings, who I thought were my blood up until the age of twelve. My adopted parents never treated me badly on purpose, but once I found out I was adopted, I noticed that I was in fact treated differently from the other children. I didn't feel remorse for any of them. Not one ounce.

I was so caught up reminiscing that I didn't even see that Amari had gotten up. He came over and sat next to me, holding me in his arms. I whispered to him that I was sorry to hear about Tanisha's death, and if he needed anything, I was there for him. I even let a few tears fall in the process, and he hugged me tighter. We took a shower together and held each other until we fell asleep.

Tanisha's home going ceremony was beautiful. She had a good turnout. Even her family members who blamed her for her parents' death showed up. I didn't know if they came to make sure she was really dead, or if they were really mourning.

The repast was held at a hall in Astoria, Queens. I made sure to help as much as I could. Amari's cousins made sure that the girls were taken care of, so that was one less thing he had to worry about.

Amari didn't feel like going back to his house, so we all went back to my place. I made sure the kids were down before I went to find Amari. I found him sitting out on the porch, drinking a beer, and I went and sat outside with him.

"I just want to thank you for everything," he said.

"No need to thank me, Amari. I love you and those girls, and I would do anything for you guys. I know me and Tanisha didn't get along, but I wouldn't wish death on anyone."

"It just hurts me that she felt she needed to take her life. I should have been there for her. I really feel like I failed her."

"Amari, please stop blaming yourself. She knew how much you cared for her, and you didn't fail her. She knew you only wanted the best for her, and that's probably why she was requesting your presence one last time, to tell you so."

He started to cry; I mean really cry. I held onto him and let him get it out.

KINDRAH

It had been two months since Tanisha passed away, and things were starting to get back to normal. Amari was back to himself, going to work while I stayed home with the girls. We talked about moving, but we hadn't decided where we wanted to go just yet. It really didn't matter to me. I would move to the moon as long as he and the girls would be there.

I decided to cook a big dinner, just to show how much I appreciated him. I got the girls ready and we were out the door, on our way to the supermarket. I decided to make macaroni and cheese, corn on the cob, and baked chicken. I also wanted to bake a devil's food cake for dessert, my favorite.

I pulled up in the Pathmark parking lot and put the twins in the stroller. I wanted to get in and get out so I could have dinner on the table before Amari walked in the door. The twins were getting restless. I didn't expect the supermarket to be so crowded this time of day. Once I got everything I needed, I checked out and was on my way back home.

Amari really enjoyed dinner, and he showed me just how much he appreciated my kind gesture, too. I needed a cigarette after that sex session. I looked over at Amari, and he was biting his bottom lip, so I asked him what was wrong.

He told me that Kelsey had been calling him and showing up to his job. She was straight stalking him. He told me that they never even had sex, so her obsession was unusual. Yes, he was cute, but who stalks a nigga based on his looks? Maybe she was stalking because she was trying to get a taste of the dick, but it was not going to happen. I hoped I was not going to have to catch a case behind this bitch. I told him not to worry about it as long as she wasn't approaching him on any stupid shit.

We watched a movie after showering. Well, the movie watched me because I was asleep as soon as my head hit the pillow.

AMARI

Kelsey was really starting to freak me out. She was leaving notes on my car window and having flowers delivered to my job. This bitch was proving to be certifiable, and I was worried. I was thinking of getting an order of protection, but that would be a bitch move. I didn't want to have to hurt the bitch and catch a case.

I told Kindrah what was going on because I promised her I would be honest with her this time around, and I meant it. Being that she was still out of work, I was thinking about us going away on a mini vacation to get away from the craziness that I had going on. Maybe if I went away for a few days, Kelsey would get the hint and disappear. I had to see if my dad would be able to keep the twins while Kindrah and I went away. I had to figure out where we would go.

As I was leaving work, I saw Kelsey's BMW parked across the street on the same side it had been on for the last few weeks. Today I decided to pull right behind her ass. I stepped out of my ride and approached her driver's side door as she rolled down the window.

"Kelsey, why are you stalking me?"

"Amari, why did you stop talking to me? I miss you."

"Listen, Kelsey, I'm sorry it didn't work out between us, but I've moved on. You have to stop with the notes and sending flowers to my job."

"Yeah, I've noticed you moved on, living with Kindrah over in your little gated community. I knew you were lying about the two of you only being friends."

"Listen, Kelsey, my personal business is no longer your concern. I'm going to need for you to fall back and stop harassing me, and I mean it. The shit isn't cute. It's crazy."

"Fuck you, Amari. You will be sorry you played with my fucking feelings when you knew you wanted to be with that bitch all along."

"Don't fucking threaten me, Kelsey. I'm trying to be nice, but fuck with me if you want." I walked off because there was no getting through to her crazy ass, and I was tired of trying.

Kindrah and I had a good time away from the madness. We didn't go far. We just ended up going to Las Vegas for the weekend, but we really had a good time. We'd been back for about a week, and I had yet to have any surprise deliveries or any visits from crazy Kelsey. I was more than happy.

Kindrah was thinking about going back to work, so we had been looking for potential childcare providers for the twins. I wasn't really feeling comfortable leaving them with strangers, because I had met my fair share of crazy people for a lifetime.

KINDRAH

Amari had been on the day shift for months now, and I was really feeling like going back to work. He was okay with it, but he really didn't want to leave the twins with strangers, so he was debating going back on the night shift. This way he would be home with the twins during the day, and they would be home with me at night.

The twins and I were on our way home from their grandpa's house, and I had this strange feeling in the pit of my stomach. It was a feeling I always got when something was going to happen, but while driving on the Grand Central Parkway I didn't see anything out of the ordinary.

As soon as I was coming around the curve to the Long Island Expressway, I was hit from behind, and my car jerked forward. I tried not to panic because I had the twins in the car, but when I was hit from behind again, I started to scream, which caused the twins to start crying. I felt one last thud as the person hitting me caused me to crash into a wall. My head crashed into the windshield, and I drifted off into darkness.

AMARI

I got a call at work, telling me to get to North Shore Hospital. The man on the phone didn't give me any information. I called my father to tell him to meet me there.

I was driving like a maniac, trying to make it to the hospital. When I arrived, I jumped out of my car and ran inside. The security officer was trying to tell me that I couldn't leave the car there, but I kept going. I saw my father, and he had my aunt with him. I asked him if he knew what was going on, and he told me that Kindrah was in an accident leaving his house, and she was rushed into surgery. He told me that the twins were okay. They had a few bruises, but other than that, they were going to be okay.

I spoke with one of the nurses, and she took me in the back to see the twins. Tania and Tiara both looked fine, and they were smiling when they saw me. I said a silent prayer for Kindrah, praying that she was going to be okay too. The doctor said that they were going to keep the twins overnight to observe them to make sure they didn't suffer any other injuries.

The nurse came and informed us that the surgeon was ready to speak with us. She took us to a room across from where the twins were placed. We all sat down to wait for him to come in and speak with us. I was nervous. My leg wouldn't stop shaking, and my dad told me to try to calm down. When the doctor walked in, I knew right away that something was seriously wrong with Kindrah.

"My name is Dr. Kanse. I'm sorry to inform you that Kindrah Watts didn't make it out of surgery. Her injuries were too severe, and she went into cardiac arrest on the operating table. We were unable to revive her. Again, I'm sorry for your loss. If you would like to see her before she is taken to the morgue, we will give you and your family some privacy."

I was numb as I fell to my knees, crying and praying that it was a mistake. My father put his hand on my back. He was trying to console me, but I was a mess.

"Son, let's go see her before they remove her," he said.

I got up and walked with my father down the hall to the room that they had her in, crying all the way. My father came into the room with me, and as soon as I saw her, I broke down. My dad was trying to be strong, but I saw the tears falling from his eyes as well. I walked over to her bed, kissed her on her lips, and exited the room.

I fell to the floor, crying and rocking back and forth. I couldn't believe she was gone. She was my everything. What would I do without her? I said another prayer, asking God to give me the strength to go on for my daughters, because right now, I didn't want to live the rest of my life without Kindrah.

It had been a year since Kindrah's untimely death, and I must say my world was turned upside down. I dedicated my life to my girls, making sure that they were well taken care of. I made sure that they always felt loved. They had lost two women who loved them more than anything, and I was going to make sure that they never forgot the love of my life, Kindrah, and their mother, Tanisha.

It is said in life that you reap what you sow. It is also said that what goes around comes back around. For Kindrah, the words she lived by were the same words she died by. Karma was a bitch, and it came back full circle.

AMARI

I stood watching Kelsey as she slept. I never thought I would allow her back into my life. When Kindrah passed away I was vulnerable, so she helped me cope with her death. She became that shoulder I needed to lean on. She became a big help to me with the girls, and they had really grown to like her.

At first, I didn't feel comfortable bringing her around the girls because I hadn't forgotten how possessive and crazy she acted in the past. I can honestly say that I had yet to see that side of her. Also, since she'd been back in my life, she had been nothing less than a blessing to me and the girls.

Kelsey was spending the night. I had a job-related function that ended later than I expected it to, so I allowed her to stay. My thoughts drifted back to how she became a part of my life again.

When Kindrah died, the first year I did everything I needed to do, like being strong for my daughters. Somewhere along the journey, I failed. I was going downhill fast. I stopped going to work and was drinking every day, without a care in the world. The girls were being passed back and forth between my dad and other family members. Tiara had gotten sick while she and Tiana were spending the night at a classmate's house, something I would have never allowed if I was myself.

Liquor had become my best friend. I needed a babysitter because I had a date with Paul Mason, but I couldn't find anyone. When the twins' classmate's mother, Lexi, who had a thing for me, asked if they could have a sleepover, I said yes.

Lexi had to rush Tiara to Harlem Hospital that night because she was having trouble breathing. She panicked the whole ride to the hospital, trying to reach me, but to no avail. Once at the hospital, the doctors started asking her questions that she didn't have the answers to. Kelsey happened to be working that night and asked Lexi if she had given Tiara anything with peanuts. Lexi told her that she had given the girls peanut butter cookies earlier that day. Kelsey let the attending doctor know that Tiara was allergic to peanuts, and she believed she was having an allergic reaction.

Lexi finally reached me on the telephone and told me I needed to get to the hospital because Tiara was having an allergic reaction. I prayed all the way there, asking God to make sure my baby girl would be okay. I promised if God answered my prayers, I would never drink again. By the time I got to the hospital, Tiara was no longer experiencing tightness of the throat or having trouble breathing. She was still showing mild symptoms, but she was going to be fine. The doctors wanted to keep her overnight, just to observe her, and if she was okay by morning, she was going to be discharged.

That night, when Tiara fell asleep, I went looking for Kelsey to thank her, but her shift had already ended. When she got to work the next day, she stopped by Tiara's room to see how she was doing. I thanked her, and to show my appreciation, I took her out to dinner once Tiara was feeling better. We'd been friends ever since, and true to my word, since that day I'd never touched another bottle of alcohol. I still indulged in my herbal medicine from time to time.

So here I was, standing over Kelsey, fighting the urge to touch her. No, I wasn't feeling her in that way, but looking at her ass hanging out of the T-shirt she was wearing had my dick responding. I hadn't had sex since the last time I slept with Kindrah, and that was over a year ago, so it was natural for my man to be jumping. Once again, I disappointed him as I pulled the cover that had fallen to the floor, and covered her body with it. I then proceeded upstairs to check on the girls, something I did every night before showering and going to bed.

KELSEY

I tried to lay as still as possible. I felt Amari's presence standing over me, and I was hoping he would touch me. I'd been waiting so long, and it had taken everything in me to play my position over the past year. It was becoming harder with each passing day because I was in love with him. I knew he was still mourning the death of Kindrah, so I was being patient and biding my time. I hoped he would eventually fall in love with me too. I made sure to be the opposite of who I really was, so it was just a matter of playing that role. I knew I deserved an Oscar because I was playing the hell out of this role. I didn't want to be nominated; I wanted to win.

Amari was still fighting his feelings as he took the blanket that I had purposely kicked off of me and covered me with it. He then proceeded up the stairs. Once he was upstairs, I sat up, smiling. It felt good to know I was finally making progress. He was beginning to feel something for me, and I couldn't wait until he stopped fighting those feelings. I knew he was still leery about me, but I had shown him nothing but love and respect. I was on a mission, and I wasn't about to get all jealous and become that person—unless he gave me reason to show my ass. Until then, I had to continue to play my position. Don't get me wrong; it was not all an act. I really did love him and his girls. It was just when I thought of Amari with someone else, or even talking to a female, it got me crazy.

I decided to lie back down because I had to be to work at 7 a.m. even though I really didn't want to go. I wanted to stay home and spend some time with Amari since it was his day off.

I didn't want to seem clingy, so when I got up that morning and was ready to go, I kissed him on the cheek and told him I would call him later.

AMARI

Once Kelsey left for work, I got the twins washed, dressed, and fed them some oatmeal. This was something I did every morning, even though the daycare served breakfast daily. I wanted to make sure that they started the day off right. I knew when kids didn't want to eat breakfast at school, they weren't forced to do so, and I felt good knowing they had the most important meal of the day.

I dropped the girls off at school and then headed to get a haircut before meeting up with my dad for lunch. The barbershop wasn't too crowded, but my barber had someone in the chair. I sat down, listening to the guys talk shit about the game that was the previous night. My thoughts drifted to Kindrah. I missed her so much. Not a day went by that I didn't think of her. I did a good job smiling on the outside, but on the inside, I was still hurting.

I had lost three women who I loved with my all. I really hated my days off because thinking of all I had lost was what my day usually consisted of. I really needed to start living again before I started getting depressed. I knew that turning to an outlet that would probably cause me more harm than good was something I really didn't need.

Clean cut and shaved, I left the shop to meet up with my dad, but I had a stop to make. I was going to Kelsey's job to take her lunch just to say thanks for keeping the girls for me the night before.

At her job, I had Kelsey paged. When she came to the front, the smile she had on her face made me feel good. I was glad I had decided to do this for her because I really did appreciate her. I handed her the lunch, and I could tell she was thankful as she gave me a hug. I told her I would call her later because I was headed to meet my dad for lunch.

When I made it to Dukes on Third Avenue, my dad was already seated, waiting on me.

"Hey, Dad. Were you waiting long?"

"No, I just got here. Let's order so we can get to the reason I asked you to lunch."

I ordered the chicken fried steak with herb mashed potatoes, honey glazed carrots, and a strawberry lemonade. My dad kept it simple, ordering a Georgia Country Cobb salad with the same drink as mine.

"Amari, I don't want to bring up your past mishaps, but you know last year wasn't a good year for you. In the midst of you trying to find yourself, the girls' birthday got overlooked. This year I want to make it up to them and plan something nice."

"I kind of figured that's what you wanted to talk about, and I think we should do it. Last year was a rough year for me, and my girls endured a lot. I think they deserve to have their day be great, so whatever you and Auntie plan will be fine," I said.

"What do you mean, whatever me and Auntie plan?" he said as he laughed.

We finished lunch and agreed to get together at a later date with my aunt to plan the birthday party for the twins. I hugged my dad, thanked him for lunch, and was now on my way home. I still had hours to kill before it was time for the girls to be picked up.

KELSEY

I was sitting in the lounge at work with a few coworkers that I was cool with. I was telling them how happy I was that Amari bought me lunch, and I also shared how I felt that I was making progress with the relationship. Out of nowhere, this bitch Rain blurted out that Amari was just using me. She said I was nothing more than a babysitter to him, and I needed to stop being so naïve.

I was taken aback because we had always been cool. I couldn't figure out why she was coming at me like that in front of everyone. I remembered when we first met Amari, she was salty because she was feeling him. She was laying it on thick, trying to get with him, but he wasn't interested and instead, he asked me for my number. I thought we were past that, but apparently, we weren't. I felt as if I was going to snap, and that wouldn't be a good look at work, so I closed my salad, wrapped my pita bread, and stood. I made sure to give Rain a look to let her know this was far from over.

I knew I scared the others because when I got upset my eye color changed, and it made me look demented. I knew that was the case because the look on their faces showed me they were seeing what the mirror has shown me on so many occasions.

I left the lounge, pissed that I couldn't get at Rain the way I wanted to. Once again, I was playing the role of someone sane. I went to the ladies' room and tried to calm down as I banged my head repeatedly against the stall door until I couldn't take it anymore. Why would that bitch say that about Amari? If he wasn't feeling me, why would he come all the way here and bring me lunch? She was a stupid bitch, and I was going to teach her a lesson that she wouldn't live long enough to teach anyone else.

***

Rain was staying at work to do a double. Everyone knew that she always went downstairs to smoke a cigarette before the shifts changed. She opened the stairwell door to proceed down the stairs, and I came up behind her, startling her. I pushed her hard enough to send her falling down the stairs. Standing there looking down at her, I could tell her neck was broken. I walked down the stairs and stood over her body just to make sure she was dead before proceeding to the parking lot to my car. I drove home, listening to my Nina Simone CD and thinking of Amari. Not once did I feel any remorse about what I'd just done.

Hours later, I sat ignoring my ringing cell phone because it was Janet calling. I refused to answer because I didn't need to be told what I already knew. I didn't feel like pretending I cared, because I couldn't care less. That bitch deserved to die. She shouldn't have stuck her nose where it didn't belong.

AMARI

After seeing the news about a woman who worked at Harlem Hospital having an accident, I began to worry. The news wasn't releasing the victim's name until her family was notified. Kelsey wasn't answering her phone, and I had a bad feeling it was her because every woman that came into my life had been taken from me. I tried to reach her a few more times to no avail. I decided to start dinner for the twins while they played in the den that I had turned into a playroom.

Once the chicken was in the oven, I proceeded to make the rice and vegetables, but not before calling Kelsey's job to see if I could get any information. Because I wasn't family, they didn't give me any, so I prayed that she was okay. It was hard to concentrate on the task at hand, which was now to give the girls a bath. I was really beginning to worry because she would have called me by now. I was trying to remember a coworker's name so that I could call her job again and try asking for one of them. I couldn't remember anyone's name, even though I had been introduced to a few of them on several occasions.

KELSEY

I sat listening to all of Amari's messages, and they warmed my heart. It felt good to know he cared and was worried about me. I wanted to dwell in the feeling of being loved, so I decided to hold off on returning his calls. After a while, I couldn't take it anymore. I needed to hear his voice.

I decided to call him back at ten that night. I told him that the reason I didn't call was because all of the employees were being questioned, and I just got home. I spoke to him for about an hour before hanging up. I went to bed that night with a smile on my face. Oh, how I loved that man, and I couldn't wait until the feeling was mutual.

AMARI

I finally spoke to Kelsey and was relieved that she was okay.
I felt bad for the woman who lost her life. I had met her a
few times when visiting Kelsey. I said a silent prayer for her
family. It was always a sad situation when a child was left
behind without a parent. Believe me, I knew the feeling, and
my children would also know the feeling.

The next day was the monthly parent meeting at the
twins' school. I always made sure I was available to attend. I
dropped the girls off to their classroom and proceeded to the
conference room where the meeting was being held. When I
walked in, I noticed Lexi, so I went and sat next to her. Lexi
seemed nervous, even though I had assured her many times
that I didn't have any ill feelings toward her about what had
happened with Tiara. She still felt as if she was to blame. I
sensed that she was still uncomfortable about the situation,
and it bothered me because she did everything right to save
Tiara. She shouldn't have felt any kind of way.

"Good Morning, Lexi."

"How are you doing, Amari? Hope all is well," she answered
nervously.

"Lexi, when are you going to stop being all nervous when
you're in my presence?"

"I'm not nervous," she lied.

"I can't tell. Just be honest. Why can't you let it go? I told
you it was my fault, not yours. You had no way of knowing
that Tiara is allergic to peanuts."

"I know. I just feel so bad about the whole situation."

"Well, don't. And just to prove to you that I have no hard
feelings, let me take you out to eat or to a movie."

"Amari, you don't have to do that. It's not necessary."

"I didn't say it was necessary. I never got the chance to show my gratitude, so I want to show you that I don't blame you. I'm grateful for how you handled the situation," I said.

"Well, since you put it that way, let me know when, and I'm there."

"Cool. I still have your number, so I will call you so we can decide when."

Once the meeting was over, we said our good-byes and parted ways.

KELSEY

I had a migraine, and I was sick and tired of hearing about the death of Rain and how distraught everyone was. I swear once I gave these two children their shots, I was taking a much-needed breather. All of the sad expressions throughout the office were making me want to just leave work. What was so special about that bitch? She was annoying and was always in somebody's business. She thought she knew every damn thing. Not to mention, the bitch felt like she was better than everybody, so I felt I did the world a favor. If I could get rid of all the Rains out there in the world, I would.

My ass was sweating bullets when I was questioned that morning. The detective calmed my nerves when he said it was being ruled an accident. It was procedure to question everyone who was working that shift.

I went to the cafeteria to get a tea and a bagel. When I got to the front, my much-needed breather was short lived as I saw Janet walking toward me.

"Hey, Kelsey, I can't believe Rain is gone. I cried all night. I told her to stay off those back steps. I hope her family sues this hospital."

Even though I didn't want to hear about Rain's ass for the hundredth time that morning, I was happy that she just confirmed that the detective was really ruling this as an accident. *Whoop-whoop!*

"It's really sad, Janet. I've been beating myself up because my last encounter with her wasn't a good one." I pretended to choke back tears as she rubbed my back. She was about the stupidest bitch. I wished she would take her pale-face ass up out of my face.

I took another fifteen minutes and told Janet's dumb ass to let my supervisor know I needed more time to myself. Shit, I might as well get on the sympathy boat if it was going to play in my favor and give me time off from the ward.

I called Amari, but he didn't answer. He was probably still at the meeting. I finished my tea and bagel and went back upstairs.

I had three patients waiting to be weighed and have their vitals taken before putting them in a room to wait on the doctor. The next day, I would be working in the nursery, and I couldn't wait. I loved working there because most of the new mothers wanted to keep the babies with them. When you had those moms that didn't want to bond with their babies at all, my ass had to do some work.

LEXI

I had just gotten off the phone with Amari. We had been talking on the phone every night for the past week. We had yet to go on our outing because my mom, who helped me when I needed a sitter, was away visiting her sister who had taken ill. I really liked him. He made me laugh. What I liked most about him was he wasn't like most men who didn't know how to converse. He was knowledgeable on so many topics, and I just soaked it all in.

I knew he'd been through a rough patch in his life and was raising his girls on his own. He opened up to me and let me know that his children's mom had passed away, and months later, his girlfriend died also. He was really having a hard time letting go and starting over. I knew he loved his girlfriend, because I didn't know many men who went without sex for that long. Yes, he shared that with me. Like I said, we'd been talking every night.

He opened up to me, and I opened up to him as well. I shared with him that my daughter's father, my boyfriend of five years, had just decided that he didn't want the relation-ship anymore. He also didn't want to be a father because he walked away from her too, never looking back. I was in a bad place, but for the sake of my daughter, I pulled myself together and took it one day at a time.

After I got off the phone with Amari, I put Imani to bed. I tucked her in and read her a bedtime story before taking a hot shower and turning in for the night.

Amari was pulling up at the daycare at the same time I was parking. We made eye contact, and I smiled. After I walked Imani to her classroom, I signed her in, spoke to her teacher for a few minutes, and then left. As I exited the school, Amari was leaning against my car door. I felt the butterflies dancing around in my stomach as I looked at the man I had been crushing on for like forever.

"Good morning, Amari."

"Hey, Lexi. Let me find out you're avoiding me."

"I'm not avoiding you. I speak to you every night on the phone, so how's that avoiding you?" I said as I tried to conceal the smile that was trying to escape.

"Well, it seems like you are, being that we have yet to go out to the movies."

"I told you my mom is out of town, and I have no sitter for Imani."

"I tell you what; let's have dinner and a movie night. You, me, and the girls. This way you don't have any excuses to be nervous, and you can stop avoiding going out."

"That's fine, but I told you I'm not avoiding you. Anyway, how's this Friday?"

"Sounds good to me. Now that that's done, have a good day at work, Lexi."

"You do the same, Amari."

I had a permanent smile plastered on my face as I drove to work.

AMARI

Movie night went well, and the kids played amongst themselves for the most part, not really interested in the movie. Lexi and I got to know each other a little more than we already did. I learned that she worked as an administrative assistant to the Commissioner of the Housing Authority. She lived on the Upper East Side, in the same home she grew up in. Her mother now resided in a condo across town from her. Lexi's father had passed away from lung cancer five years earlier, and she finally convinced her mom to move on a year ago. She met a nice man that they all adored, and she married him eight months after meeting him.

When her mom remarried, she didn't want to live in the home that she and Lexi's father had shared. She didn't want to taint the love she shared with Lexi's father by bringing another man to live there. I only hoped that I would find happiness again. It was really hard to move on, but I was now ready to try.

Lexi and Imani left around ten that night. It was way past the twins' bedtime. As soon as Lexi left, I bathed them and put them to bed. My phone chirped, indicating I had received a text message.

Lexi: I made it home safe. Thanks for tonight. I had fun. Imani's behind didn't want to leave. LOL.

Amari: I had fun too. Hopefully we can do it again.

Lexi: I would love to do it again. I will call you tomorrow when I get back from Imani's dance class.

Amari: Dance class at two years old?

Lexi: LOL. Yes, my baby has been in dance since the age of one, and she loves it. You should think about signing the twins up.

Amari: Wow! Maybe I'll check it out.
Lexi: Okay, have a good night.
Amari: You do the same.
Lexi: Thanks.

KELSEY

It was one of those days that I wanted to sleep in, but unfortunately, it was not going to happen. I was doing a shift change. Janet had agreed to switch her Saturday for my Tuesday so that I could spend the day with Amari on his day off next week. No, he hadn't invited me; I wanted to surprise him with a matinee movie and lunch at Ruby Tuesday.

I had tried calling him a few times last night only to reach his voice mail. It was unlike him, but he must've turned in early.

Work wasn't busy at all that day. I really liked working the Saturday shift. They had me working with Dr. K, prepping his patients for GYN appointments. His ass was fine. I'd always been attracted to the light-skin, pretty-boy type, but this dark chocolate man, standing at six feet of fineness, had my thong moist. I hadn't had sex in so long waiting on Amari, but Dr. K's ass could definitely get it. I'd been flirting all morning, and his ass was acting all professional and shit.

After his last patient, all that professionalism went out the back door. He had my ass lying on the examining table with my feet in the stirrups, fucking the shit out of me. He was working my insides, taking me to a place I hadn't been in a minute. I closed my eyes and imagined it was Amari putting this work in as I tightened my pussy muscles. He pumped in and out of me with so much intensity. I cried out Amari's name over and over. He didn't seem to care as he continued to assault my pussy until he came just as hard as I did.

I went to the bathroom to clean myself up. When I walked out, Dr. K tried talking to me, but I continued walking. How crazy was that? I was attracted to him, and I wanted to fuck him, but he wasn't Amari. I was not going to be satisfied with anyone, even if the dick was good. I now knew that it was a waste of time trying to get that much-needed release because I was still going to feel empty inside if Amari wasn't the one doing the releasing. I needed Amari like I needed to breathe. I felt dirty and couldn't wait to get home to wash the scent of another man off of me. How could I have been so stupid and cheat on Amari, the love of my life? I needed to be punished. This was not acceptable.

When I got home, I sat in a tub of scalding hot water. It burned my skin. I felt like I was on fire, but I deserved to hurt. I sat in that tub, apologizing to Amari until the water went cold and I was satisfied that I had cleansed myself of another man.

LEXI

I was sitting at work when my coworker came in all smiles, carrying a bouquet of flowers. Jealousy was written all over my face. She was always getting gifts from her boyfriend, like every week, and it made me sick. To my utter surprise, she handed them to me. When I read the card, I was really shocked. I must've made an impression on Mr. Amari. I was all smiles as I texted his number because I knew he wasn't able to talk at work.

Lexi: The flowers are beautiful. Thank you so much.

Amari: I'm glad you like them. I wasn't sure if you could receive deliveries since you worked with the commissioner, but I took a chance because I wanted to send them just because.

Lexi: Wow, I feel so special. No one has ever sent me flowers. This means so much to me.

Amari: I'm glad I got to be the first.

Lexi: LOL. I'm glad you got to be the first, too. Thanks again. TTYL.

Amari: Yes, you will. You're welcome.

Oh my God. I had tears in my eyes. That little gesture meant so much to me. My coworker, Shelly, was standing there waiting for the 411, but I dismissed her. I didn't need my business being talked about all over the office. I also didn't want to put too much into this because he never said anything about a relationship. We were only friends, even though I wanted more. I'd always had a crush on him, but since we'd been spending time together, I was falling for him. Until I knew he was feeling the same way, I was going to keep my feelings to myself.

My phone alerted me that I had a text message, and when I saw it was from Amari, I smiled so hard I felt like I cracked my lip.

Amari: Hey, I'm off tomorrow. Do you think you could play hooky and be my guest on an outing?

Lexi: I would love to. Let me check with my supervisor. I'll get back to you and let you know if I can get the day.

Amari: Cool, let me know.

I was all smiles again and tingling all over. I'd only had this feeling one time before, and that was when I fell in love with Imani's father. This was too soon to be feeling this way, wasn't it? This was scary. I just hoped I don't get hurt having these feelings so soon for a man that I hadn't known long.

It was easy feeling this way about him because he always made me smile. He checked on me to make sure I was okay, and he seemed to only want the best for me and Imani. I felt myself falling hard. I just hoped he'd be there to catch me when I fell.

AMARI

I dropped the girls off to school early so that I could get back to the house before Lexi got there. She was going to drop Imani off at her regular time and then drive to my place so she could park her car. We had agreed to take my car. We didn't have to pick the girls up until 6:00 p.m. I had to pay extra for that 7:00 a.m. drop off, but it was worth it to me. It took me a long time to even think of entertaining a woman, let alone falling for one. Lexi had come into my life and had me falling for her, and it felt good.

I heard the doorbell ring, so I figured it was Lexi. As soon as I opened the door, the smile left my face because it was Kelsey and not Lexi.

"Hey, what are you doing here?" I asked, trying not to show the irritation in my voice.

"I came to surprise you. I have the day off, and I wanted to take you to the matinee and lunch."

I tried to get my words together so they wouldn't come out wrong. If I didn't have plans, it wouldn't have been a problem, but I did have a problem with her showing up without calling first. Before I was able to address it, the doorbell rang again. I prayed Lexi didn't get the wrong idea and didn't think that I lied to her when I said I wasn't seeing anyone.

I opened the door, and Lexi stood there looking at me with her beautiful brown eyes and a questioning look on her face. I took a deep breath. This whole scene was beginning to feel like déjà vu.

"Kelsey, this is Lexi. Lexi, this is Kelsey." I stuttered a little. Even though I was guilty of nothing, it didn't stop me from feeling like I had done something wrong.

Lexi spoke, remembering Kelsey from the hospital, but Kelsey didn't say anything.

"Lexi, could you wait for me in the living room? I'll be there in a second."

"No problem," she responded.

When Lexi was in the living room and out of sight, I tried my best to speak without sounding rude.

"Kelsey, I have plans. Had you called and let me know that you wanted to hang out, I would have rescheduled my plans," I lied.

"Well, it wouldn't have been a surprise if I called, now, would it?" she asked sarcastically.

"Well, I apologize. We can do this another time," I said, hoping she would leave without an argument.

"Fine, Amari. I will call you later," she said as she turned to leave, walking out the door.

I could tell she was upset, but what did she want me to do? She didn't call, so I couldn't feel bad about it. I went into the living room where Lexi was patiently waiting.

"You ready to go?" I asked, hoping she didn't change her mind.

"Let's do it," she said as she smiled, letting me know we were good.

Finally a woman who wasn't for the arguing about nothing. I was pleased about how she had handled the situation. I just had to find a way to make Kelsey understand that she couldn't just be popping up at my crib without calling. Whether she was trying to surprise me or not, this whole situation could have gone left with Lexi if she had been that girl. You know, the one that goes off, no questions asked. I grabbed my car keys and we were on our way out the door.

KELSEY

I sat in my car and tried to calm my nerves. I couldn't believe what had just happened. I was confused. When did he start seeing the bitch that almost killed his daughter? *Amari, really?* It took everything in me to continue playing my role and not go off. I'd come too far to mess it up now.

I didn't want them to see me still sitting in my car, so I just started to drive, no destination in mind. I'd be damned if I put in all this work for someone to come and take Amari from me. Amari's ass had gotten a pass on so many occasions because I loved him, but if he thought he was going to lead me on again, just to up and leave me for the next bitch, he would feel what all of the others felt. If I couldn't have him, no one would.

I wasn't always this way. It all started when I was fourteen years old. Derek, my mom's boyfriend, who at twenty-eight was ten years younger than her, was always attentive to me. He would buy me things and help me with my homework, basically doing all the things my mom never had time to do. My dad had walked out on us when I was nine years old, and my mom was never the same. It was like she blamed me because he no longer wanted to be in the home. All the love and attention went down the drain, along with cooked meals and putting clothes on my back. She began running the streets, dealing with man after man, who were all no good. They used her for sex and for somewhere to lay their heads.

When she met Derek, I thought he was decent enough. Why he decided to deal with my mom, I had no idea. She treated him like shit and barely made time for him. Derek and I became really close, so close that I started to mistake his actions toward me as his wanting to be with me.

One night, he was staying over and Mom had already turned in. I sat down on the couch with him and began watching the movie. I placed my hand on his thigh as I started to massage his penis through his pants. He pushed my hand away and jumped up from the couch like his pants were on fire. I asked him what was wrong, and he began screaming at me. He told me that I was just a child and asked what in the hell would he want with a child. He yelled how he was a grown-ass man, and I should be ashamed of myself for acting like a slut. I started crying, seeing red.

He tried to soften the blow by telling me that I was beautiful and that I needed to concentrate on being a teenager. Boys would come later. He continued by saying that I didn't need to throw myself at grown men because the next man just might respond in a way I would regret. Yada, yada, yada.

He made the mistake of turning around and heading toward my mom's room. I reacted because I thought he was going to tell my mom what had happened. I grabbed my trophy off the table and hit him two times in the head. He fell back and hit the table. My mom ran out in a panic when she heard the glass shatter.

When she saw Derek, she started screaming at me, asking me what I did. It made me even angrier that she never asked me why I did it. She automatically went to his aid. The bastard started moving, letting me know I didn't hit his ass hard enough. My mom was now on the phone dialing 911.

When they arrived and began wheeling his ass away, I spun a story to the police that landed his ass in jail for ten years. From that day on, any man that rejected me got dealt with in some form or fashion. I was not about to stop at Amari's ass.

I gave myself a headache traveling down memory lane, so I decided to go home. I thought about following Amari, but until he said that he was not trying to be with me, I still had to play my position, so I took my ass home.

LEXI

I really enjoyed my time with Amari. He took me to the matinee. When he held my hand, I thought I was going to faint. His touch had me feeling excited, and I felt myself getting moist again. After the movie, we had a nice lunch at Outback. I wanted to ask him about Kelsey, but I didn't want to ruin the mood, so I let it go. He didn't give me a reason to question him. He had been nothing short of a gentleman.

Amari drove to the school, picked up the girls, and we took them for ice cream before I picked up my car and we parted ways. I drove home feeling good about everything. Amari and I were really beginning to feel each other. He admitted it, so I decided to be honest and let him know how I was feeling as well. We both agreed to take it slow to see where it went. He did open up on his own and told me that he and Kelsey used to date, but they never had a sexual relationship. He said he broke up with her because she became very possessive. They were only friends now and had been friends since the incident at the hospital. He mentioned that she had been a big help with the girls, and he appreciated her, but that was the extent of the relationship.

I believed him. I really had no reason not to at this time. If he had any type of relationship with her, she would have made it known, especially after seeing another female in his home. She didn't speak to me, but I just took that as her being upset with me about what happened with Tiara.

Once I got home, I sat with Imani to help her with her homework sheet. Once she finished, I made dinner. Tonight, she and I were having movie night. I tried to have movie night with her at least once a week, getting our quality time in, and she loved it.

Amari was on my mind heavy. I forced myself to focus on the movie until my phone chirped, indicating that I had a message. Music to my ears.

Amari: WYD?

Lexi: Movie night with Imani.

Amari: No invite?

Lexi: LOL. No, just me and mini me tonight. Maybe next time.

Amari: :(

Lexi: Awww, I'm sorry, but you had me to yourself all day. It's li'l mama's turn.

Amari: LOL, true. Get back to li'l mama. Good night.

Lexi: Good night.

Amari and I had been hanging out every weekend, sometimes with the kids, but most of the time it was just us. I knew it was soon, but I was falling in love. He was everything I wanted in a man and more.

I was starting to think the commissioner was getting jealous with all the deliveries I received. I swear Amari was a sweetheart. He was like no other man I ever met. I prayed this was the real deal. I really didn't think my heart could take another hit like it did when Allen walked out on me.

I had just gotten done with my invoices for the day. While I was clocking out, I felt a cold chill like someone was standing behind me, but when I turned around, no one was there. Sometimes I hated being the last one to leave the office. I held my flowers and rushed to my car. I didn't feel safe until I was inside with my doors locked.

I drove to the daycare listening to my Mary J Blige CD, thinking about Amari. I wasn't going to see him at the daycare center because he didn't pick his twins up until 6:15, but at least I got to see the girls, who I had grown to love.

KELSEY

Once again, I was at work stressing. I felt like Amari had been giving me the cold shoulder the past few weeks. Not once had he asked me to pick the girls up from school for him. I had been picking them up on the days that he got mandated to work. I knew for a fact that he'd been getting mandated because I'd seen that bitch picking them up on several occasions, and that didn't sit well with me at all.

On top of that bullshit, Janet told me that Dr. K had been calling almost every day, trying to speak with me. He even asked her to get me on the phone when she worked with him on Saturday. I spoke to him one time and told him that I was in a relationship, and that day in the examining room was a mistake. That didn't stop him from continuing to try to get in contact with me. I felt like the tables had been turned. The shit that he was doing to me was what I did with a few of the men I stalked. I just hoped he didn't become a problem.

On my break, I decided to text Amari just to see if we were still good.

Kelsey: Hey, Amari. I haven't spoken to you. Just checking to see how you and the girls are doing.

I decided to take the next patient while I was waiting for him to respond. This wouldn't be the first time working on my fifteen-minute break.

By the time my lunch hour came, Amari still hadn't replied, so I chalked it up as him not having a signal at work. By the time I got off at 5:00 p.m., he still hadn't replied, and I was getting pissed off. I drove to the daycare to see if he would be picking up the girls. I saw him pull up to the school, and I watched as he went inside, got the girls, and put them in the car. He was just sitting in the car, so I decided to call him.

He sent the call to voice mail. I figured he sent me to voice mail because he was getting ready to pull off, but he continued to sit in the car. Why would he not answer my fucking call? He was probably sitting there texting that bitch.

Oh, wow. Fifteen minutes later, this bitch and her fucking daughter exited her car and got into Amari's car. He pulled off, and I waited a few minutes before pulling out to follow him.

Oh, no. I knew that he fucking wasn't pulling up to his father's house. I felt like I couldn't breathe as my heart broke into a million pieces. He was taking this bitch and her daughter to his dad's house. He had to really be feeling this bitch. He never took me to any of his family members' houses. I mean, I met most of them at the twins' first birthday party, but that was not the same. My feelings were truly hurt. I really felt stupid as I thought back to what Rain had said about him. She was right; Amari don't give a shit about me because if he did, he wouldn't have been disrespecting me like that.

I decided to text him. Maybe I was reading too much into this. It could possibly be innocent.

Kelsey: Hey, Amari. Did you get my text earlier?

Amari: Hey, Kells. Yes, I got the text. I was pretty busy today. I just got home with the girls, so let me get them settled and I will ttyl.

Kelsey: Okay.

That lying motherfucker! On my life, he was going to regret loving me and leaving me this time. I was going to destroy his life, starting with taking away anyone who meant something to him.

I pulled off, screeching my tires as I ran the red light, not caring about anything or anyone. My thoughts were consumed with making Amari hurt. I didn't mean the hurt he felt losing Kindrah; he was going to relive the pain he felt when he lost his mother. When he became vulnerable again, I'd be right there pretending I cared, just to shatter his perfect world some more.

Make no mistakes, I loved Amari, but sometimes you have to take drastic measures to let motherfuckers know that you're not to be fucked with. I should've just stayed behind and waited for them to get into the car and then rammed into them again and again until the car was totaled and everyone inside was dead. It took everything in me not to turn my car around and go back. The unwanted tears escaped my eyes as I thought of them inside of his dad's home with him expressing his love for this bitch and her child.

Knowing how I felt about him and how he felt about me— well, at least that's what I'd led myself to believe. Why didn't he love me? I had been there for him through it all. I saved his daughter's life, and he chose the bitch that almost took it from her. What kind of repayment was this?

Once home, I didn't even bother to turn on the lights. I sat on the couch, rocking back and forth, trying to keep the crazy inside of me calm. I was trying to avoid doing what I needed to do hastily. This had to be a well thought out plan. The rocking back and forth was a calming mechanism taught to me by one of my many doctors, and it seemed to be working as my eyes got heavy. Lying on the couch, I closed my eyes, falling asleep with a heavy heart.

AMARI

As I got the twins ready for school the next morning, I couldn't help but think of the good time we'd all had at my dad's house the night before. My dad loved Lexi, and Imani was a hit with him. I told him how I felt about her, and he told me to go for it.

I powered on my phone and noticed that I had a few missed calls from Kelsey. I'd had to power it off the night before because if she wasn't texting me, she was calling. I knew I had told her I would talk to her later, but that didn't mean to keep calling me just because I didn't call. Something could have come up. I just hoped the crazy in her wasn't about to resurface again. I would hate to have to unfriend her again; but I would. The last thing I needed was to be dealing with that kind of behavior when I was trying to start a new relationship. I didn't know if Lexi will pursue a relationship with me if Kelsey began to act possessive like she had done in the past.

After dropping the girls off, I went to do some much-needed grocery shopping since it was my day off. I also needed to go and pay a few bills, then off to Lexi's job to take her to lunch.

I loved how close Lexi and I had become. After lunch my mind was made up. I wanted to do something nice for her. I called her mother and asked her if she would be able to keep the girls for us because I wanted to surprise Lexi with a weekend getaway for just the two of us. I was thinking about taking her to the Poconos. It was time for me to stop holding back and give her all of me. Kindrah would always hold a place in my heart, but there was room for me to love another.

Lexi had taken the rest of the day off to spend it with me. She was lying down on the couch, watching *Divorce Court*. She was supposed to be home with me chilling, but for the past hour she had been giving daytime television all of her attention.

"Hey, what happened to spending the day with me? You've been neglecting me," I said, trying to hold my laughter in.

"I'm sorry. It's just I'm never home to watch daytime television, so I got a little sidetracked. What's up?"

"I was thinking we should get your mom to keep the girls this weekend so we can have some alone time."

"That sounds nice. So it's just a matter of getting my mom to watch the girls. Why are you smiling that goofy smile?"

"I'm smiling because I already asked her. She said she would keep them. Poconos, here we come."

She jumped in my arms and hugged me and then pulled away quickly, as if she did something wrong. I pulled her back into my arms, and we shared our first kiss, one that I was enjoying very much.

I started to feel guilty, as if I were cheating on Kindrah. I had to remind myself that I promised to give her my all. So I put my all into the kiss to let her know that I was definitely feeling her.

I was first to break the kiss because I also wanted to show her that I wanted more from her, not just a quick fuck. I looked into her eyes, and I saw the love. I knew I was doing the right thing by planning this trip to take our relationship to the next level.

"You know you're not like any other man that I've ever met. I know I said it before, but it's the truth. You always seem to amaze me," she said.

"You sure you're not stuck on this New York swag I got going on? Or is it that kiss I just laid on you that got you caught in your feelings?" I asked.

"Nah, the kiss was just a'ight," she said, mimicking what she felt was street slang. It was cute.

I grabbed her and pulled her on top of me. I kissed her again, stopping when she was getting into it.

"Why you stop?" she asked.

"Tell me my kiss was the bomb and you want another one."

"Whatever."

She lay back down on the couch, and I held her from behind. We spent the rest of the day, in that spot, watching daytime television until it was time to pick up the girls from daycare.

LEXI

"Meeka, girl, I'm in love."

"Girl, go ahead with that. It's been like what, three days?" she said, laughing like I'd told a joke.

"I'm serious. I know that it hasn't been that long, but I feel like God has finally answered my prayers and sent me my soul mate."

"More like your bed mate."

She was really cracking up, thinking this was funny, when I was being serious.

"Meeka, would you be serious for a second? We haven't even had sex yet. The other day was our first kiss. This isn't just a physical attraction. I fell hard. He's everything I've always wanted in a man, and he treats Imani just like he treats his girls. You know Mom doesn't like anyone I've been with, but she loves Amari and the twins, so that has to count for something."

"Okay, so on a serious note, if you think this is your soul mate, go for it, but make sure you're not just rebounding or trying to fill a void. From what you've told me, both of you have been heartbroken for two different reasons. I don't want you jumping into a relationship built on the comfort of a man. With that being said, if you believe that he can give you his all with still having love for his deceased girlfriend, then go for it. I will support you no matter what."

"Thanks. I love you girl," I said, hugging her.

"I love you too. Now get off of me with all that mushy shit."

I loved my crazy best friend of ten years. She knew what I had been through, and I understood her being a little skeptical. She was the only one that hadn't met him yet. I wanted to wait before I had them meet, because her ass would've scared him away. Now that she knew how I felt about him, they could meet. She was still going to go in, but not as bad.

I couldn't help but laugh to myself as I thought about them two going at it. She was not going to have a chance to give him the third degree. She was going to love him. He was as real as they come. Soon he would belong to me.

"Are we going to the nail salon or not? You sitting here daydreaming about Amari's ass," she said.

"I'm ready. Let me grab my bag."

When we got to the nail salon, it wasn't crowded at all. While I was sitting in the chair getting my feet done, I got that strange feeling again like someone was watching me. I looked over at Meeka, who was sitting across from me, and out of the corner of my eye, I saw Kelsey sitting near the window, just staring. I mean straight staring, no hello, just staring dead in my face.

Meeka picked up on the frown on my face and followed my gaze. "Who the fuck is that bitch, and why the fuck she looking at you like that?"

"Meeka, shush. That's the girl I told you that was at the hospital that night and told the doctor Amari's daughter was allergic to peanuts. She also happens to be a friend of Amari's."

"Okay, and again, what the fuck is she looking at? If the bitch isn't going to speak, she needs to turn her fucking head. That bitch looks crazy as hell, but she got the wrong fucking one to be getting crazy with," Meeka said.

All I could do was laugh at my silly friend. It was not that I was scared or anything, but Kelsey had me feeling uncomfortable. It was like she was trying to get a reaction out of me, but I didn't have one to give her.

I got up to go sit at the nail station to get my nails done. Kelsey got up and bumped me as she walked by. I saw this bitch was in her feelings that day, and I didn't have time to be out there dealing with this childish bullshit. I was a grown-ass woman, but I couldn't let it slide.

"Excuse you!" I yelled.

"No, excuse you. Watch where the fuck you going."

"Look, little girl, I don't have time for whatever your problem is with me."

"My problem with you is you're fucking rude, and you almost killed Tiara. I helped your ass out, and you never apologized.

Now you're sniffing your stink ass around my man. Now you know what problem I have with your ass," she said.

"So Amari's your man? Not only are you young acting, but you're delusional, too. And for the record, I thanked your ass the same night. Please don't stand here and blame me for something I had no knowledge of."

"Whatever. You're a dumb bitch, and you need to stay away from Amari."

Meeka was sitting calmly, and I knew it was just a matter of time before she got up. I tried to defuse the situation, but it was too late. She was already up in Kelsey's face.

"Hold the fuck up, bitch! You need to back up out of my friend's face. She has too much class to go back and forth with this bullshit, but I don't give a fuck. I have no problem mopping your ass across this floor."

"I would love to see your Amazon-looking ass try," Kelsey said.

I already saw where this was going. I didn't want to see Meeka's ass in handcuffs, being hauled off to jail. It was sure to happen because these Koreans were now talking in their language. One of them was on the phone, so we needed to leave.

"Meeka, let's go. She's not worth it," I said.

"Yeah, listen to your friend before I—"

She never got the chance to finish her sentence. Meeka punched her in the face, and she fell to the floor. Meeka started stomping her. The shop owner was screaming in her language into the phone. I grabbed Meeka, who was on ten by now. I had to drag her out of the shop and force her into the car. I hightailed it out of there.

"Why didn't you let me finish giving that bitch the business? That bitch doesn't know who she's fucking with. Got me out here fighting in flip flops."

I burst out laughing. This girl was off her rocker.

"Meek, I told you to leave it alone. She's not even worth it."

"She called you out your name one time too many. I knew your working-for-the-commissioner's ass wasn't going to show out, so I handled it for you. What's up with this bitch claiming Amari?" she asked.

"She on some bullshit, but I will be speaking to his ass about her claiming him."

"I'm tight right now that I didn't get my nails done. I have a date tonight."

"Well, we can go somewhere else if you want," I said.

"Nah, I'm good. Just take me home before I catch a case in these streets."

"Whatever. Your ass crazy as hell," I said, laughing.

"Nobody fucks with my sister from another mother."

"Thanks, sis."

After I took Meeka home, I picked Imani up from my mom's house and drove straight home. I couldn't wait to let Amari know about this girl and the scene she caused in public.

After Imani was fed and sitting quietly watching television, I texted Amari.

Lexi: Hey, Amari. Are you busy?

Amari: Nah, what's up?

Lexi: I need you to give me a call if you can talk.

Amari: Okay. Give me a few minutes. Let me put the girls down.

About twenty minutes later, I ran to answer my phone. "Hello."

"Hey, it's me. What's going on?"

"Well, you know I took off to hang with my girl Meeka, right?"

"Yeah."

"Well, we go to the nail salon on Clinton to get our nails and feet done. I'm sitting in the chair getting my feet done, and I look up and Kelsey is in the far corner just staring at me. She didn't say hello or nothing, just sat there staring at me. I started to feel uncomfortable, so Meeka asked me who she was and why was she staring. I told her to just ignore her. When my feet were done, I was walking over to the nail station to get my nails done, and Kelsey walks towards me and bumps me. So I'm like excuse you, and she goes off, telling me her problem with me is that I almost killed your daughter. Now I'm sniffing around you—her man—and I better stay away from you.

"She kept calling me out of my name, and I refused to stoop to her level, but Meeka is one of those no-nonsense females who can take but so much. So they started arguing, and Meeka punched her in the face, and she fell to the ground. I grabbed Meeka, got in the car, and we left because the owner was on the phone calling 911. I didn't need my friend going to jail for that nonsense that Kelsey provoked."

"Are you serious? First off, I apologize, and like I told you before, I don't blame you for what happened with Tiara. Kelsey was out of line, and as far as her putting claims on me, she's either stupid or stuck on stupid. I have been nothing more than a friend to her, and I promise you I will deal with it. Please apologize to your friend for me."

"Amari, you don't have to apologize for her. Trust me when I say I don't believe anything she said about you being hers. I have spent almost every day with you, so that's not an issue as far as I'm concerned. I just don't have the time or the patience to deal with childish little girls. I have an image to uphold," I told him.

"I feel you. I will definitely handle it. Are we still on for this weekend?"

"Without a doubt. I'll talk to you later."

"Later, beautiful."

"Good night," I said, laughing.

AMARI

Words couldn't begin to explain what I was feeling when I got off the phone with Lexi. I had never hit a female in my life, but the way I was feeling, I could really slap Kelsey for the bullshit she started. I had let her back into my life, and this was how she did me, getting jealous and possessive all over again. From the beginning she knew that all I wanted from her was a friendship. I hated to have to fall back from her again, but after what she had pulled the other day, it may be necessary. I refused to have her destroying what I started. It took me an entire year to even entertain the thought of opening up and loving again, and I would not let her take that from me.

I had planned on doing some shopping for my getaway that weekend, but now that had to take a back seat until I saw this chick and found out what the hell had possessed her to go at Lexi.

I pulled up to the hospital, parked, and went inside to have someone page Kelsey. Her coworker informed me that she hadn't come to work that day, and that was when I remember the fight. Damn, I should have known she wasn't going to work that day.

I sat in my car and called her, and she answered the phone on the first ring like she had been expecting my call.

"Kelsey, you want to tell me what happened yesterday? Because I'm confused," I started.

"Look, Amari, the first time I saw you with her I held my tongue, but seeing her yesterday triggered something in me. I don't like her, and I wasn't going to pretend I did. She almost killed your daughter. I don't understand how you're smiling all up in her face and going on dates, chilling with this bitch."

"First off, Lexi is not to blame for what happened to Tiara. It was my fault. Lexi had no idea my daughter was allergic to peanuts. What you did was out of line. Any issues or misconceptions you have, you should have brought them to me."

"Are you serious? I'm the one who's been here with you and for you. Once again Kelsey has to play second position, and I'm sick of it. I've been to you what you always wanted me to be, and now that I'm that person, it's still not enough. Once again, you picked the next bitch."

"Kelsey, you're bugging right now. So you're really going to act as if we didn't have a conversation about me only wanting a friendship and you agreed?"

"Yes, we had that conversation, but it was because of how I acted in the past. Since I've been back in your life, I've been nothing like that person. I loved you then, and I love you now. Yes, I get crazy when I see you with someone else, but that's a normal reaction."

"Let's keep it real," I said. "If you loved me, we would still be in a relationship. You never showed me love. All you showed me was craziness and possessiveness. True, you changed, but I don't share the same feelings you have, because you never gave me a chance. When you resurfaced, I made it clear that all I wanted was a friendship. I finally found someone who I want to be with, and you almost destroyed it for me. So I'm going to tell you, if you don't think you can handle me being in a relationship with Lexi without causing problems, I'm going to have to fall back and ask you to do the same."

"Wow, really? After all I've done for you, this is how you do me? So you trying to tell me that this past year you've felt nothing for me? You could just fall back because of someone you just met, and you've known me for two years. It's that easy for you?" she asked.

"I don't want to fall back, but if you can't continue to just be my friend without all the extra stuff and respect who I chose to be with, then yes, I have to fall back. If you love me like you say, then you would fall back too."

"If I only loved you like a friend then we wouldn't even be having this conversation. I would have no problem seeing you happy, but I love you as more than a friend. I don't want to lose you again. This isn't fair. What's wrong with me that no one loves me?"

I didn't know what to say as she began crying. I kind of felt bad that she was crying. Like I told her, I had no idea she was developing feelings for me. If she had shown me anything other than friendship, I would have told her I wasn't interested.

"Kelsey, are you still on the line?" I asked.

I could still hear her crying, but she didn't answer me. Just as I was about to hang up, she spoke, and she wasn't crying anymore. Her voice had changed.

"Amari, all I ever wanted was for you to love me the way I loved you, but to no avail. I tell you what: not only will I fall back, but I promise to make you feel the same pain you caused me to feel." She hung up the phone.

I didn't usually scare easy, but she sent a chill through my body that had me a little worried she would do something stupid.

Friday I was making sure that I packed everything the girls would need for their stay with Lexi's mom. She was picking the girls up from school, so I needed to take the bag to the school. I was confident that all would go well. They had spent the night with her a few times before, and she was aware that Tiara was allergic to peanuts, so I wasn't worried.

After the girls were dropped off, Lexi and I were on our way. I had decided against going to a resort. I planned a stay at a bed and breakfast inn, a cozy and intimate setting in Paradise Valley. During the ride up, we listened to the radio and talked about all the things we wanted to do. I could tell Lexi was excited about getting away, and so was I.

We stopped for breakfast. Neither of us had a chance to eat that morning. I had to turn my phone off the night before. Kelsey's calls and text messages were getting on my nerves. Some of the threats were crazy.

I pulled up to the inn a little after noon. We made good time.

The room had a homey feeling to it. We had a fireplace, Jacuzzi, and a big-ass king-size bed. The only thing I wasn't feeling was that the bathroom was located outside of the room and shared with everyone who occupied rooms on the second floor.

We decided to unpack later. We both wanted to go to Mount Airy Casino. I had thought about staying at their resort, but it was more of a resort for established relationships. If you were planning to have your wedding ceremony, then that would be the spot, but we were only interested in a little gambling.

Lexi went straight to the slots, and I hustled over to the blackjack tables. I wasn't really a gambling man, but I enjoyed it once in a while. After losing a few hands, it was time for me to go. I went back over to where Lexi was playing the slots.

"Hey, are we rich yet?" I asked.

"No, I'm down and ready to go," she answered.

"I guess we both suck at this gambling thing."

"Let's go back to the room and have some fun in the Jacuzzi," she suggested.

"Okay, let's go."

We walked out of the casino, hand in hand, smiling.

I sat in the Jacuzzi waiting on Lexi. When she walked back in the room and dropped her towel on the bed, she had on a two-piece red bikini. My dick was on full alert as I leaned back in the Jacuzzi and watched her as she stepped in. We played in the water like two kids as we splashed each other, not caring that we were wetting the floor. She never complained about her hair getting wet. That was one of the things I loved about her. She was so laid back that she made it easy to love her.

All that touching each other had me ready to take it to the next level. "Come here, Lexi," I said, licking my lips.

"What can I do for you, Mr. Amari?"

"You can bring your sexy ass over here and let me taste those lips of yours."

"You have to be a little more specific. I have two sets of lips," she said as she splashed me with water and tried to run to the other side of the Jacuzzi.

I grabbed her and turned her around to face me. Our lips touched as I parted hers and slipped my tongue in her mouth. Our tongues got familiar with each other for the second time, but something about this time was different. There were more feelings, more emotion involved.

We both opened our eyes, just staring at each other. My eyes were asking her if she was ready to take our relationship to the next level, and her eyes were saying yes.

I lifted her up out of the Jacuzzi, stripped her of her bikini, and stood back, taking in all of her. She was flawless; her body was beautiful. She had firm breasts, a small waist, curvy hips, and an ass that screamed to be touched as the water glistened on her milk chocolate skin.

I wasted no time getting on my knees and tasting her. I put both hands on her round, plump ass as my tongue made love to her insides. She was trying to keep her balance. As she was losing control, her nails dug into my scalp. She screamed out that she was coming as I swallowed all the sweet juices that she released into my mouth.

I picked her up, carried her to the bed, and gave her a minute to catch her breath before I flipped her on her stomach to give her ass crack a dick massage. I wanted to let her feel what I was working with. She moaned loudly, letting me know she was enjoying it, and I removed my dick and replaced it with my tongue. I was licking up and down her ass, opening her legs slightly as my tongue double-dipped inside of her. My fingers rotated on her pussy lips in a circular motion until she was screaming my name.

Once she came again, I reached for a condom, this time not giving her a chance to catch her breath. I entered her gently, pumping in and out of her slowly, trying not to ruin our first time even though I hadn't had sex in what felt like forever. Her being wet and tight didn't help the matter, as the sensation was taking me over the top.

She tightened her pussy muscles as she began twerking on my dick. I lost it, pumping harder in and out of her. She yelled loud, a little too loud, that she was coming. I pressed my lips against hers to quiet her down just a little as we had an explosive orgasm together. I collapsed on top of her with my dick still inside of her, wishing I could stay in her hotbox forever.

I kissed her on her forehead as I lifted my body weight up off of her. I lay on my back and pulled her into my arms, where we both drifted off to sleep in that position.

EDWARD

Tired and exhausted from a hard day at work, all I could think of was taking a hot shower and going straight to bed. I had hung out with Ana at the bar the night before, knowing I had to work in the morning. I'd had a good time but paid for it all day with a banging headache. Tonight, my bed was calling me, and I was answering that call. My partner had been kind enough to let me drive the truck while he picked up the trash, but I knew he was not going to keep doing me that solid. I was taking my ass to bed to get my body right for lifting in the a.m. We were scheduled to work the Lower East Side, so no doubt it would be a lot of trash lifting. The regular sanitation guys always slacked in that area.

I pulled up in my driveway. Finally, home sweet home. I walked into the living room and clicked on the light. Sitting on my couch was Kelsey, with her legs crossed, gun in hand, with a smirk on her face.

"Kelsey, what are you doing in my house?"

"Oh, so you remember my name. Last time we spoke, my name was bitch."

"Why are you here? I told you I never said anything to Amari or anyone else, for that matter. Now please leave."

"Cute, trying to give orders when I'm the one holding the gun."

I tried to remain calm, but she was beginning to really piss me off. This bitch made my life a living hell for eight months then disappeared and reappeared at my granddaughters' birthday party with my son. She then had the nerve to threaten me that she would hurt my son if I ever told him about her crazy ass.

I had met her deranged ass at the gym, where I thought she was a well put together young lady. Boy, was I wrong. That was what I got for trying to get my groove back. These young females were very possessive, but Kelsey took the cake. She was possessive and a grade-A stalker.

I was snapped back to the situation at hand when I heard her cock the gun.

"Kelsey, what the hell do you want?"

"I'm here to talk about the visitors you had the other night. It seems you're into helping your son cheat on me. What kind of man are you?" she asked.

"Wouldn't he have to be with you to cheat on you?"

"Again, cute. Your son loves me. You can sit here and pretend like he doesn't, but I know the truth. We were fine until this bitch and her daughter came and ruined us. I saved his fucking daughter, and he cheats on me with the bitch that almost killed her. Then he has the audacity to tell me I need to fall back."

"Wow, you're crazier than I thought," I said. "You need to stay away from my son and my grandchildren. I should have never agreed to not telling him about you."

I reached for my phone. I was going to put an end to this today. Amari needed to know who he was dealing with. I went to dial his number, and that was when I felt the first bullet hit me in my chest. I knew she was off her rocker, but I never thought she would shoot me. I dropped to my knees as I felt the second bullet hit me in my shoulder. My chest was on fire as I began gasping, falling face down onto the floor. I closed my eyes and said a silent prayer to God to protect my son and my granddaughters as she stood over me and shot me two more times in my back.

AMARI

Lexi and I were still lying in the same spot. I didn't even realize we had slept that long, missing dinner in the process. I gently lifted her off my chest as I got up to answer my ringing phone. I looked at the phone just to make sure it wasn't Kelsey calling. I saw my dad's number on the caller ID.

"Hey, Dad. What's up?"

"Hello, I'm trying to reach Amari James," said a voice I didn't recognize.

"This is Amari. Who is this?"

"Mr. James, this is Detective Jerome. My officers responded to a call from a neighbor who reported hearing gunshots coming from your father's home. I'm going to need you to meet me at Jamaica Hospital."

"Is my dad okay? I'm out of town and it's going to take me at least two hours to get there."

"Mr. James, is there anyone else you can have meet me at the hospital until you're able?"

"Yes, I'm going to call his sister, and I will be there soon."

I was calm talking to the detective, but when I got off the phone, I was a mess. I called my aunt to let her know what was going on and to have her meet the detective at the hospital. Lexi was already getting into her clothes upon hearing the call.

I was a nervous wreck not knowing if my dad was okay. Lexi handed me my clothes, and while I got dressed, she grabbed the bags along with the keys to drive. I was in no condition to drive. The more I thought of the call, the more the tears started flowing. I didn't care how I looked, crying in front of Lexi.

Her eyes watered while trying to convince me that everything was going to be okay, but we both knew that it wasn't going to be all right. I just hoped that he wasn't hurt too bad.

AMARI

It took us a little over two hours to get to the hospital. As anxious as I was to get there, now that we were sitting in front of the hospital, my legs wouldn't move. I feared the worst.

Walking into the hospital, I felt like my legs were going to give out on me. All of my family was posted up in a private room, awaiting the doctor. My dad had been shot once in the chest, once in the shoulder, and twice in the back, and he had lost a lot of blood. He wasn't conscious when they brought him in, but he was breathing. He was now in surgery, so all we could do was pray; and pray is what I did.

I cried for Tanisha, Kindrah, and now my dad. The pain was unbearable. That's when Kelsey's words rang out loud and clear.

I wondered, *Could she be responsible for shooting my dad and leaving him for dead? Just because I didn't want to be with her, would she go to this extreme? That's insane, but at the same time, too much of a coincidence.*

My phone alerted me that I had a text message. It was from Kelsey, and it read:

ASHES TO ASHES, DUST TO DUST. ARE YOU SURE FALLING BACK IS STILL A MUST?!?!?

I felt sick that I may have been the cause of my dad being shot down like a dog. He didn't deserve this. Why would she do this? I swore she was going to pay for this, and she had better pray to God my father pulled through.

Just as I was going to let my uncle know who I thought was responsible for my dad being shot, my phone rang. It was my neighbor who lived across the street from me, telling me that my house was on fire and she had called 911. I didn't want to leave my dad, but I had to go.

"Lexi, I need you to drive me to my house. My neighbor just called and said that my house is on fire."

"Oh my God! Could this night get any worse? What the hell is going on?" she asked.

"Well, I believe Kelsey is behind my father getting shot and my house catching fire."

I filled Lexi in about Kelsey's threats to hurt me the way I had hurt her by rejecting her for the second time. I also showed her the text message that she had just sent.

"Amari, you need to call that detective and let him know what's going on. This is crazy. What kind of person does something like this because they were rejected?"

"Someone who's crazy and feels they have nothing to lose. I don't want to believe she did this, but all the evidence points to her. But I will say she better pray that the police catch her before I do. I have never in my life felt like hurting anyone the way I feel like hurting her."

"I understand how you're feeling, but let the authorities handle this. You don't need to be in anyone's jail when you have Tiara and Tiana to worry about," she said.

We rode in silence the rest of the way to my house. I was really hurting for my dad. He didn't deserve this. He wouldn't hurt anyone. He would give you the shirt off his back if you needed it.

When Lexi pulled up to my house, I had no words as I watched the firefighters try to save my home. My tears of anger were hard to stop as the chief of the fire department spoke to me. He basically told me what I already knew: the fire wasn't an accident, and they would be conducting a full investigation.

If Lexi wasn't there with me, I swear I would have drunk myself into a coma just to numb the pain for a little while. My mom, Tanisha, Kindrah, Dad, and now my home. I didn't know how much more I could take before I said fuck this life. Lexi tried her best to console me, but at this point, I was inconsolable.

I gave the detective all the information that I had on Kelsey, which wasn't much. All I knew was her name, where she used to live, and her job information. I had no up-to-date address, no family members, nothing. I felt so stupid to have trusted her again.

Once back at the hospital, I got a little hope. My dad was out of surgery, but not out of the woods yet. He was still unconscious, but breathing on his own. That was all God.

We stayed the night at the hospital with the hopes of seeing him, but the doctor informed us that my father wouldn't be able to have visitors until later on that day. We decided to go see the girls and come back later. I wasn't up to the task of facing my girls and letting them know we no longer had our home and Grandpa was hurt.

I got a call from the detective. He said Kelsey was a no-show at work, and the address the job had on file turned out to be an abandoned tire shop.

LEXI

I felt like I was in the Twilight Zone. I was away with the man I had fallen in love with, and we were enjoying each other's company. After enjoying some of the best sex I'd ever had, we had fallen asleep in bliss only to wake up to a nightmare.

Who would have thought Kelsey was certifiable, straight fucking crazy? I thought about the incident at the nail salon and wondered if she would come after Meeka. We knew nothing about this bitch.

I didn't understand how Amari had her around his kids and did not know where she laid her head. I'm not saying it was his fault that he assumed she still resided at the home she used to live in, but it was his fault for trusting her crazy ass again after the signs she showed him in the past.

I tried calling Meeka to give her a heads up, but the call went straight to voice mail. I was in deep thought, trying to figure out how could I tell Amari I was scared and thought it was best that I fall back. My life and my child's life were more important to me than sticking around in hopes of Kelsey being arrested and placed in custody.

Did they really have enough evidence to arrest her? I mean, all he had was a text message and a threat that only he heard. So who was to say she would be off the streets? If she did commit these crimes, that meant she did all of this because she couldn't have him. Who do you think she blamed? Who do you think she would be coming after? I had no problem protecting myself, but how could I fight against a ghost? She disappeared; she could have been watching us at that moment for all we know.

When Amari was done talking to the doctor, I was going to tell him, but looking at him so broken, I couldn't find it in my heart to do it. How could I blame him for her actions if I was going to be with him? I had to be there for the good and the bad. I just hoped it doesn't cost me my life.

We stopped at Walmart to pick up some underclothes, a few pair of jeans, and some shirts for Amari before heading to my mom's house to pick up the girls. Amari and the girls were going to be staying with me until he figured out his next move.

I was kind of nervous, because if crazy-ass Kelsey was following us, she would know where I lived, and that meant I would be putting my daughter in harm's way. I was also putting my mom in danger as well. I should have had her meet us at the mall with the girls.

"Hey, Lexi, I know what you're thinking, and trust me when I say I wouldn't put your family in harm's way on purpose. If you need me and the girls to stay somewhere else, I will understand," Amari said.

"Amari, I'm not going to lie and say I'm not nervous or afraid that I might be putting my family in danger, because I am. But I will never turn my back on you in your time of need. After what Imani's dad did to me, I never thought that I would feel what I feel for you with anyone again. You made it easy to love you, and I'm going to be here for you."

"You love me, Lexi?"

"Yes, I love you, Amari James. I know we haven't been together long, but like I said, you made it easy."

"I love you too, Lexi, and if you feel that it's best to walk away from this crazy situation that I put you in, I would understand. It will not change my feelings towards you."

"Amari, you're stuck with me, and I'm not going anywhere. We just have to be careful of our surroundings until they find Kelsey. We also need to get a 'No Pick Up' list at the school. If it's not you or I, no one is allowed to pick them up."

"We can do that in the morning, and once I get the report from the fire chief, I can file my home insurance and find a place before you get sick of me," he said.

"Never," was my reply.

When I pulled up to my mother's house, Amari exited the car. I jumped into his arms and kissed him, not wanting to let him go. I swear this feeling that I was feeling I hadn't felt in so long. It was the feeling of new love developing into something real.

I didn't like the look on my mother's face when we walked in, so I left Amari and the girls in the living room to go see what the look on her face was about.

"Lexi, baby, I don't know what's going on, but what I do know is that I will not put my grandchild in danger. You know how I feel about Amari and his girls, but I care about you and Imani more. I refuse to stand back and watch you continue in a relationship while he has a jealous ex-lover who's running around recklessly," she said.

"Mom, this girl is no ex of Amari. She was a friend who wanted more than he was willing to give, and she went crazy. She shot his father and set his house on fire all because he started seeing me. It's not fair for me to turn my back on him. He has no one else," I lied.

"Lexi, do you hear yourself?" she yelled.

"Yes, Mom, I do. I understand your concern, because I'm scared that I'm getting in way over my head, but I can't walk away even if I wanted to. I love him."

"Lexi, you're playing a dangerous game. You better be careful. This girl is crazy, and I will never forgive you if something happens to my grandbaby."

"Mom, I will never let anything happen to my baby."

She walked out of the kitchen. No more words were said. When I got to the living room, the girls were watching cartoons. Amari was no longer with them. My mom had spoken to me, and I assumed that my stepdad was speaking to Amari. It was a setup.

They came from the den, smiling, so that was a good sign. It seemed their conversation went better than the one I had with my mother. Amari smiled at me, and I smiled back, and just that quick, my mood changed.

We got the girls ready, and just as we were walking out the door, my mom called out, "Amari, can you please take the girls to the car?"

I sat on the couch, not really up to hearing anymore about the situation. I loved my mom, and I knew she meant well, but now really wasn't the time to try to convince me to walk away.

"Lexi, I just want you to be safe. Take this." She handed me a black case.

I was hesitant because I had an idea what it was, but I took the case and opened it up. It was the Taurus PT-22 handgun. I was familiar with the gun. It was the same gun she always kept for protection.

"Mom, I can't have a gun in the house with children."

"Lexi, I'd rather you be safe than sorry. You'll have to find a safe place in your home just as I did."

I put the case in my pocketbook. I knew if I said no, she was going to make me bring Imani back into the house because she felt like I couldn't protect her. I wasn't a stranger to guns. My dad had taught me how to shoot at a very young age. As I got older, our Saturdays consisted of target practice. I just didn't like the idea of a gun in the house with children.

KELSEY

Janet called to let me know that two detectives had come to the job looking for me. She said they left a card, asking that I give them a call. I wasn't interested in no fucking detectives, because nobody was going to stop me. Amari could send the troops if he wanted to. It still wouldn't stop me. Only thing that would stop me would be him calling me and telling me what I needed to hear so that we could be the family we were supposed to be. I was not done playing games with his ass yet.

Now that I couldn't go to work, I decided to go stake out Lexi's house. No doubt that would be where he'd stay. I called his job, and they said he hadn't been in, so maybe I could catch him there without Lexi being around.

I pulled up to Lexi's house just as Amari was pulling out of the driveway, so I decided to follow closely behind him. Because I was in a rental, I didn't worry about him being on alert. He would never expect me to be following him in this piece of shit car. He knew I was high maintenance and wouldn't be caught dead in a Toyota.

Amari pulled up to his father's house and parked in the driveway. I was assuming he was there to clean up the mess I'd left. I parked, got out of the car, and waited ten minutes before going toward the house.

I looked through the window from outside, and sure enough, he was cleaning up the living room. I turned the doorknob. To my surprise, he hadn't locked the door. I walked in like I owned the place. He turned around, and the look on his face scared me just a little, because I'd never seen him this angry before. He had good reasons, but I had good reasons for my actions, too.

"What the fuck are you doing here, Kelsey? I know you're crazy, but stupid, too? Not a good combination."

"No need for name calling, Amari. All I want is to love you. Why can't you see that? Why do you continue to make me do bad things, Amari?"

"Kelsey, you're sick. I don't know how many times I have to tell you that all I want from you is your friendship, but you just don't seem to get it. Why can't you understand I don't have any romantic feelings towards you?"

"So you're really going to stand there and tell me you feel nothing for me? I find that hard to believe. Whenever it's just us, you treat me like a boyfriend treats a girlfriend, but as soon as you meet someone, you want to put me on the back burner. You did it with Kindrah, and now you're doing the same thing since you met Lexi," I said.

"It's not even like that. All I tried to do was be your friend. All I asked was you be my friend in return. It never fails. You have to go and get crazy every time someone enters my life, so don't blame me when I don't want to be bothered with you anymore," he said.

"Amari, I love you. I've always loved you. I never loved you just as a friend. Don't act like you didn't know how I felt about you. You've been stringing me along all this time until you found someone else. Everything I do is for you and because of you. I even killed for you."

"Like I said, you're sick. So you're telling me that you're responsible for my dad being shot and my house being burned down all because your crazy ass couldn't have me? What the fuck is wrong with you? All of this over some dick!"

I stood looking at him with a smirk on my face because it was clear that he didn't understand that this had nothing to do with dick. I loved him for him, and I was willing to do whatever I needed to do to have him and prove to him how much I really loved him.

He must've gotten tired of waiting on me to answer because he was now in my face. He slapped me so hard I lost my balance and fell to the floor. I looked up at him in disbelief as I started sliding backward to get away from him.

"Kelsey, I'm going to ask you one more time. Did you shoot my father and burn down my fucking house, you stupid bitch?"

I still said nothing as he grabbed me and began ripping my shirt.

"So you're still not going to answer me? This is why you shot my dad and burned down my house, bitch. All because you couldn't get any dick? You want this dick so bad that you will kill for it? Is this what you want, bitch?"

I started to regret leaving the gun in the car. I never thought that Amari would hurt me like this. I started to fight back, but he was too strong as he forced my pants down and then my panties.

"Amari, don't do this," I yelled, but he continued. As much as I loved him and wanted to have sex with him, I didn't want to have it like this. He was hurting me. "Amari, please," I pleaded to no avail.

"Don't cry now, you stupid bitch. You felt no sympathy for my dad or my home when you burned it down, leaving me and my girls homeless. You had no remorse when you sent me text messages thinking the shit was funny. Now who gets the last laugh, bitch? You take this dick since you say you love me so much."

Amari had his hands tightened around my neck and was choking me as he pumped in and out of me with so much force. He was hurting me, and the tears just poured from my eyes as I stared into the eyes of the man I loved with my all. I began losing consciousness as he continued to pump inside of me. With each pump, his grip around my neck tightened, and I welcomed the darkness.

AMARI

Oh my God. What the fuck did I just do?

I blacked out. One minute I was having a heated conversation with Kelsey, and the next thing I knew, I had slapped her. The rage had a mind of its own as it took over.

I looked down at her. She wasn't moving, and she was bleeding between her legs. I began panicking as I tried to wake her up, but she didn't move. I began to regret putting my hands on her. I should have just called the police and let them handle it, but like I said, I couldn't control the anger that had built up in me over the past few days. Looking at her as she just smirked at me like it was a joke that she shot my dad and burned down my house had done something to me.

I had just wanted her to pay for what she did. I didn't want her blood on my hands. I had my girls to raise. Now I might have put raising my girls at risk because I stooped to Kelsey's level.

I thought about cleaning up all the additional blood that was now soaking into the floor. *Oh, shit! What about me not wearing a condom?* When they did find her, my DNA would be all over her.

I couldn't breathe. I needed some air, so I grabbed my keys off the table and left. I started to feel sorry for her. I had never wished harm on her, even after what she did. I still had some kind of feelings about leaving her to die. I thought of my daughters and decided that I was going to make an anonymous call to the police station. I changed my mind as soon as I thought about my dad lying in that hospital bed and me being homeless.

I drove straight to Lexi's house to change clothes before it was time for me to pick up the girls. I couldn't get the scene of me choking and raping Kelsey out of my head. I had no idea if she was dead or alive, but secretly, I was praying she was dead.

I was wondering if I should tell Lexi what happened—leaving out the rape, of course. She wouldn't even begin to understand my mindset for raping her. I wouldn't be able to explain what possessed me to rape her, as opposed to just killing her.

When Lexi got home from work, the girls and I were sitting in the den, watching television. I got up, kissed her on the lips, and asked her to put her things away so she could meet me in the kitchen.

"What's up? You look stressed," she said when we were alone.

"I think I killed Kelsey. I went to Dad's house to clean up. I was in the living room when I heard the front door open and close. I turned around, and Kelsey was standing there."

"Oh my God! What the fuck was she doing coming back to your dad's house?"

"She had to be following me. She knew he wasn't going to be there. So anyway, we start arguing, and she tells me that she loves me, and she has even killed for me."

"Are you serious?"

"Yes, very serious. So I asked her if she shot my father and burned down my house. She didn't answer. She just had this smirk on her face, and I lost it. I slapped her and began choking her until she wasn't moving anymore."

"Did you call the police?"

"No, I panicked and left the house," I admitted.

"We have to go back. If she's dead, we have to get rid of the body if you're not going to go to the police," she said.

The only thing stopping me from agreeing with her was the fact that Kelsey was naked from the waist down. How would I explain her being exposed?

"I don't know about going back and getting you involved in murder. It's too risky."

"Amari, I told you we are in this together. I'll be damned if I let the police find her and charge you with murder. Now, let's get the girls ready. We will drop them at my mom's. We will have to tell her that we are going to the hospital to see your dad."

Shit, I was nervous and worried at the same time. When we got to my dad's house, reality sunk in as I looked at Lexi. She looked scared. We were in way over our heads, but we couldn't back out now.

I held her hand as we walked up to the house. Once inside, I was at a loss of words. The living room was cleaned, like an attempted murder or rape hadn't happened at all. Kelsey was no longer lying in the spot I had left her in. We searched up and down my dad's home. She was not there.

"Where the hell is she?" Lexi asked.

"I have no idea. This place was a mess, and she was lying right here," I said as I pointed to the spot she was in when I had left.

"Well, she couldn't have been dead."

I sat on the couch with my head back, trying to figure out how this was possible. The bitch was dead. Well, I had thought she was dead, but apparently she wasn't. This shit just didn't make any sense.

"Babe, let's go. I'm getting the creeps," I said.

I locked up my dad's place, and we left to go pick up the girls. I was still at a loss for words, so the ride to Lexi's mom's house was quiet as I played all kinds of scenarios in my head as to what the hell had happened at my dad's house. If Kelsey wasn't dead, how the hell did she get the strength to scrub blood off floors and put everything back in its rightful place? If she was dead, who moved the body and cleaned up the living room? I was really getting a headache trying to figure shit out.

Back at the house, my stress level was on ten. Fresh out of the shower, I retired to the den just to clear my head.

"Hey, babe, are you going to be okay?" Lexi asked.

"I'm good. I just gave myself a headache thinking about what the hell happened back there. The not knowing is killing me."

"I know how you feel. I haven't stopped thinking about it either. The million-dollar question is, do we still have to look over our shoulders?"

"Lexi, I don't know what to think at this point. Clearly something went down at my dad's house, and we have no way of finding out what happened after I left."

Once Lexi went to sleep, I sat up, deep in thought, trying to figure this shit out. I even called Kelsey's phone to see if she would answer, but the call went straight to voice mail. I called all the local hospitals, but she wasn't a patient at any of them. This shit was mind-boggling. Eventually, I drifted off to sleep.

KELSEY

I tried to adjust my eyes to the light that was shining in from the window. I had no idea where I was. I knew that I was in a basement, but who had put me there and why? Last I remembered, I was being beaten and raped by Amari. Just the thought had tears falling from my eyes. How could he do me like that? All I tried to do was show him how much I loved him and how much he meant to me.

I tried to move, but my body was sore, and it hurt each time I attempted. I still felt the dried blood and semen between my legs. I swore if I got out of this situation, Amari was going to pay.

I heard the basement door opening and then someone walking down the stairs. The only light was coming from a small window. I really couldn't see the face of the person who entered. I was thrown a bottle of water and a sandwich wrapped in plastic.

"Hello, who are you? Why do you have me locked in this basement? Please. I need to get out of here. Who in the fuck are you, and what do you want with me?"

I tried to get up to lunge at the person only to get pulled back. Not one time had I realized I was confined to a bed. I cried out as the door opened again, letting me know I was being held by more than one person. This shit was unreal. I fucked with others' lives, not the other way around. Who was bold enough to fuck with me?

I wished I had some pain medication. My face hurt, and the pain between my legs was unbearable. I needed to soak in some bath water, but I didn't think it would be happening anytime soon.

DR. K

"You didn't say that kidnapping was going to be a part of the plan," I said.

"Well, plans change. She wasn't supposed to be raped and left for dead. If I knew she was weak, I would've gotten rid of her a long time ago, being I have to finish the job. I need her alive to take the fall. Had the police found her, the case would have been closed. She wouldn't be blamed for the job that I have to now finish," my partner answered.

"So how is this going to play out in my favor? What do I get out of this now?" I asked.

"Don't go getting soft on me. Plans change, like I said. Just be happy you get to live and continue your career."

"Don't threaten me! This shit is really getting out of hand. I would love to see the infamous Amari James. Maybe I will get a better understanding of why he has so many bitches going crazy over his ass."

"Watch your fucking mouth, K, and don't underestimate me. I will have your ass floating face up in the fucking East River. Go make sure the basement door is locked so we can go."

This bitch was really starting to get on my fucking nerves. Even if the basement door was unlocked, how would Kelsey get out? She was tied to the damn bed. I didn't know how I had let myself get into this situation.

I'd always had a weakness when it came to the opposite sex, and once again, it had gotten me in a fucked-up situation. Now I was stuck on this dumb-ass mission and didn't know how to abort. This bitch had me by the balls. This bitch could get me arrested on so many charges, including falsifying documents and deleting medical records. If I got arrested, that would be the end of my career, and she knew it.

I hoped she was about to go on one of her stalking outings. I have five patients scheduled that day. I looked forward to them, just to get away from her crazy ass for a few hours.

As soon as I walked through the hospital doors and onto the elevators, I breathed a sigh of relief. Finally, a break from all the craziness that had gotten out of control. I was secretly thinking about putting in for a transfer and getting out of dodge.

When I first met her, I had really believed that she was a damsel in distress. I had my brother, who was her attending doctor, to assist me with what she was requesting. At the time, it made sense, but now I saw that the wool had been pulled over my eyes. My brother and I could face serious jail time. None of it made sense anymore.

My brother had no idea that she was fabricating, and I still had yet to tell him. If and when I did, he would probably advise me to go to the authorities. Clearly, I was in way over my head and didn't know how to stop this madness.

LEXI

Amari and I had been doing well. He finally got his check from the insurance company, so he was now looking for a place of his own again. I really didn't want him to leave. Imani and I had gotten used to our extended family, and we loved them. If they were to move out now, it wouldn't be the same without them. I enjoyed waking up to Amari next to me every morning and hearing the children running and playing, enjoying each other. Imani loved having sisters in the house. Those were her words, not mine, but I felt the same way.

I wanted him to stay, but I wanted him to want to stay. I really didn't know how to approach the subject. We were now en route to my mom's house for Saturday dinner. Maybe that night, after the girls were asleep, I could bring it up and see how he felt about it. I knew for sure I was going to miss making love to him every night if he left. For that reason alone, I had to get him to stay. I had fallen deeply in love with Mr. Amari James. His lovemaking skills and how he spoiled me and the girls were an added bonus.

I'm telling you, I had so many haters at work since I met Amari. It was a damn shame that they liked me more when I was walking around always depressed after Imani's dad dumped me. Oh yeah, as long as I was miserable, they loved being in my face. My misery made them feel so much better about their fucked up lives.

"Why is my boo so quiet over there?" Amari asked.

"Your boo is just thinking about something. Nothing really important."

"I can't tell. It must be important. Had you in deep thought. You didn't even hear Imani calling you." He laughed.

"I'm sorry, Mani. Mommy was just thinking about something."

"She's not paying you any mind now. Is it something you want to share?" he asked.

"Yes and no, but I'll wait until we get home tonight and the girls are asleep."

"Oh, you want me to put it on you again? You were thinking about last night?" he joked.

"No, I wasn't thinking about last night, nasty man."

I couldn't stop laughing. Amari was a nut at times. He always made me feel better. I didn't know why I was scared to ask him not to move. I truly believed he felt the same way I felt about him. He probably thought he was being a burden, which was not the case. I would be sure to tell him that night that I loved him, Imani loved him, and we didn't want him and the twins to leave.

We got to my mom's house. As soon as the girls were taken out of their car seats, they ran up to the door, leaving me and Amari like we hadn't all come together. I knew why they were so anxious to get inside. They knew my mom always had something sweet for them.

Dinner was great. We were all nice and full by the time we were ready to go. We left right after the girls were done with my mom's strawberry cheesecake. As much as I loved my mom's cheesecake, I didn't have any room for it, so Mom wrapped it for me to take home.

Once home, I made sure all the doors and windows were locked. I'd been doing that every night since the Kelsey incidents. I had to say it wasn't a good feeling, not feeling safe in your own home. I went to join Amari in the den.

"Hey, baby girl. You ready to talk?" he asked.

"Well, it's not really a talk. I just wanted to ask you something."

"Ask away."

"I just want to know how you would feel about you and the girls staying with me and Imani," I said.

"You mean live here on a permanent basis?"

"Yes, silly. We're a couple. I love you, you love me, and we both adore each other's children. I say let's do it."

"Are you sure, Lexi? I don't want you to feel that you're obligated because you're my girlfriend."

"I don't feel obligated. I love you, and I want you and the girls to stay."

"Okay, the girls and I will stay," he said.

I was ecstatic that he agreed. If he had decided to get his own place, I would have really been a little shook with just Imani and me there alone. Even with the gun in the house, I still wanted him there. He made me feel safe at night.

Mondays always had me feeling sluggish in the morning, not wanting to get out of bed, but skipping work that day wasn't an option. The director was having a budget meeting, and I needed to be there.

Amari had returned to work. He had to leave at six that morning, so it was just me getting the girls ready for school. I pulled myself out of bed so that I could get our morning started.

Work was really stressful. I had a killer headache, and I just wanted to get home and soak in a tub of hot water. I was going to relax a little before Amari and the girls got home.

Leaving work, I got that feeling again, like someone was watching me, but when I turned around, just like the last time, no one was there. I hurried to my car. On the windshield, there was a note. I grabbed the note and opened the car door with shaky hands while looking around. Once in the car, with the doors locked, I still didn't feel safe. I wasn't going to feel safe until I pulled out of this underground garage.

I decided it was time for me to start carrying the gun in my purse. This feeling was getting really eerie, knowing someone was watching. The fact that they saw me and I didn't see them was enough to scare the shit out of me.

I had almost forgotten about the note. I unfolded the note, but nothing was written. It was just a picture of two baby girls taped inside. The girls looked to be about a year old. They kind of looked like Tiara and Tiana, just a younger version. I was confused about why someone would post a picture of twin girls on my windshield. This shit was really becoming child's play to me, and I was getting sick of it.

Amari had beaten me home. He and the girls were sitting in his favorite place, the den, and he had a stressed look on his face. He signaled for me to follow him to the kitchen, our meeting spot when we didn't want to talk in front of the girls.

"What's going on, babe?" I asked.

"I don't want to alarm you, but when I picked the girls up today, Imani handed me this," he said as he handed me the same picture that I had found on my windshield.

"Amari, this same picture was on my car when I got to the garage at work. Is this a picture of Tiara and Tiana?"

"It looks like them, but I don't remember the outfits. I racked my brain trying to remember, but I couldn't. I studied the picture a little more, and the little girl on the left has a mole that neither of my girls has, so I don't know who these children belong to."

"So this means someone got near the girls, and this scares me. Did you question the teachers at the school?" I asked.

"Mrs. Kenya said that another school visited the school for movie day in the auditorium, but just children and the teachers. No parents attended."

"Amari, this shit has got to stop. If anything happens to one of our girls, I don't know what I would do."

"I know, babe. I will keep the girls home tomorrow. I'll drive you to work and pick you up until we figure something out," he said.

"Maybe we can just let the school know what's going on. You can even call the detective to get some protection at our home and the girls' school until this shit stops," I said.

"Nah, I'll let him know what's going on, but I got you and the girls. If I have to take and pick you up every day, that's what I will do, including staking out at the girls' school."

"Thanks, babe, but you just got back to work. You shouldn't have to keep taking off. I can't believe God finally sent me my savior and someone's trying to destroy it."

"It's not you. It's me who came to you with a tainted background. I knew that Kelsey was off, and I invited her back into my life and my home. Granted, I didn't know she was deadly, but she should've never been allowed around my girls a second time," he said.

He continued, "I want you to trust and believe that I'm your savior, and I'm not going anywhere. God sent me what he felt I needed, and that's you. I love you, and I'm not going anywhere. And don't you worry about work. They know of the situation. My family comes first."

"Awww, you're making me cry."

"Don't cry. Wipe those tears and give me a kiss, you big baby."

"Not funny, big head."

"Yeah, I do have a big head," he said as he grabbed himself.

"Nasty, I'm going in the den with the girls before you start something we can't finish."

He gave me a quick kiss before walking away to watch a movie with the girls.

KINDRAH

Come on, pick up the fucking phone.

I was really losing it trying to get in touch with K's ass. That bitch Kelsey was in there crying that she was in pain, and I couldn't call 911.

"Hello? Hello?"

"Hello, Kindrah. What can I do for you?"

"K, you need to get your ass here ASAP. This bitch is in here screaming at the top of her lungs that she's in pain, and I need you here before I kill her ass."

"I'm on my way," was all he said as he hung the phone up.

I swore if he didn't get his ass there and find out what had her in so much pain, he was going to wish he had never met me. His ass was a doctor and he had said she was fine, but now this bitch's screaming was driving me insane. I was about to shoot this bitch in the head, not giving two shits about her taking the fall for my doings.

I opened the basement door and yelled down the steps for that stupid bitch to shut up, only for her to scream louder.

As K was coming in a little while later, I was headed out. I couldn't stand to be in the house another second with all of the screaming she was doing.

"Make sure you shut that bitch up. I'm out of here. That bitch done drove me crazy."

I watched as he made his way to the basement door. I wanted to make sure he put on the ski mask to hide his identity, then I left to get to the place I called home.

I was happy as I walked in the house to see my baby girls smiling at me as they ran to greet their mama.

"Hey, Mommy's babies. Were you good girls for Auntie Meeka?"

"I'm not their goddamn auntie or their goddamn babysitter. I'm supposed to be your fucking girlfriend, but you got me in here being everything but that, while you're out there chasing this fuck boy," she complained.

Why couldn't this bitch understand that everything I did was to get back with Amari? Yes, I gave her the impression that my babies' daddy had left me and I was into women now. I led her to believe that I just needed her to help me get back at him, but that was far from the truth. She didn't know that I needed her ass to be a pawn in my game because her best friend was now fucking with him. I had used her as a means to get the information I needed to get this plan moving. Since it was about to come to a close, her ass was as good as out of my damn life. Amari and I would have no room for stragglers trying to get what belonged to him.

I went into the kitchen to fix my girls a snack to hold them over until dinner was done. As I began to cook, I thought back to how I had lost Amari to begin with.

I remembered being in a car accident on my way home with Amari's twins, Tiara and Tiana. I had blacked out but regained consciousness as the paramedics were yelling and screaming to each other. They were saying that I was bleeding out from a wound caused by the broken glass. I said a prayer for God to help me, and I prayed that the girls were okay. They were screaming at the top of their lungs, and I didn't know if they were hurt or just scared.

Once I was at the hospital, I was rushed into surgery. I didn't know what happened in surgery. All I knew was when I woke up, I was in a secluded part of the hospital. I couldn't move. I was in a lot of pain and hooked up to a few machines, but I didn't know why. I was drowsy, and I wondered where the hell Amari was and if the twins were okay.

I tried turning my head to look toward the door, but my body was hurting all over, and I had a pounding headache. I remembered closing my eyes, trying to get some type of relief, but I drifted off into a peaceful sleep.

When I finally woke up, I was in a state of shock. My hair had grown so long, way past its normal length. My stomach was huge, and I no longer had tubes or machines hooked up to me. The room I was in was cozy. It kind of favored a hotel room, but it was still in the hospital. I needed answers, and I needed them now.

I tried to get out of bed, but my belly made it really hard. I lay back down, and I believe I tried to get up too fast, because it felt like the room was spinning. I felt lightheaded as I looked for a nurse's station button to try to get someone in there to tell me what the hell was going on.

I didn't see anything, not even a phone. I moved slower this time, moving my feet off the bed first. I slowly sat up as I held onto the mattress. I wanted to make sure I didn't lose my balance, because I was still lightheaded.

I sat for a few seconds before sliding my body off until my feet hit the floor. I didn't stand right away. I just leaned against the bed until it was safe to stand.

"Ms. Watts, what are you doing?" I heard as the door to the room closed.

The voice sounded very familiar as my eyes followed the sound of the voice.

"Dr. Kaufman, is that you?" I squinted to get a better look. Sure enough, it was the same doctor who had treated me when Tanisha caused me to have a car accident. He was also the doctor who treated me when I had blacked out from complications from that accident.

"Dr. Kaufman, what's going on? Why am I here, and what happened to me?" I asked as I pointed to my stomach.

"Well, first, I'm going to need you to get back into bed. Only then will I tell you whatever you want to know."

I was hesitant at first, but if I wanted answers, I needed to get back into bed. So that's exactly what I did—with his help, of course.

"Where should I begin?" he asked.

"How about you start from the beginning?"

"Well, let me ask you this first: Do you remember anything?"

I told him how I remembered being in another car accident, coming to the hospital, and being rushed into surgery. After surgery, I was in a hospital room in a secluded area, and that's all I knew.

"Okay, so I will start from there. I was on call at the hospital the evening we got the call about the ambulance en route with a female who was in a car accident. She had suffered head trauma and possible internal bleeding, and she was bleeding profusely.

"When the ambulance reached the hospital, you were placed on the gurney to be rushed into surgery, and that's when I recognized you. While you were in surgery, I was talking to a colleague of mine. I let him know that this was your second car accident, and I believed somebody was hurting you on purpose. I honestly believed that they weren't going to stop until they successfully killed you.

"We agreed that we were going to protect you by hiding you and telling your family that you didn't make it out of surgery due to your injuries. We didn't know who was trying to kill you at that point, so we felt we were doing what was best.

"I had my brother, who worked in the morgue, help us pull this off, and he supplied the funeral home with a body. We moved you to a private room on the north side of the hospital, where they were doing renovations. You began to have complications. I believe we moved you too soon after surgery, and that led you to slip into a coma.

"When I logged into your medical records to erase them, I noticed that one of the tests showed an extremely high hormone level, so I administered a blood test. The test confirmed that you were pregnant. Because you were in no condition to make a decision to carry or terminate, I brought in a GYN doctor, who is a friend of mine. He monitored you the entire pregnancy because you were pregnant with twins and a high risk patient. As you can see, he did an excellent job with you, because you're about ready to pop." He laughed; I didn't.

I was livid as I started screaming and crying at the same time.

"How could you hold me against my will and lie to Amari that I died in surgery? How could you do this to me, especially after finding out I was pregnant? Who gave you the right? You have no idea what you've done! Do you know what I had to go through to finally get him to tell me he loved me and wanted to be with me? You destroyed my life, the life he and I would have had raising our children and being a family."

"Ms. Watts, I'm going to need you to calm down. Think about your babies," he said.

"Fuck you. Did you think about my babies when you told their father I died in surgery?" I tried to get off the bed, screaming at him. I thought about how I was going to report him and that he would never practice medicine again when I got finished with him.

Just as I got closer to him, I felt the needle being pressed into my arm from behind, and then darkness. When I woke up, there was no sign of Dr. Kaufman. I was experiencing so much pain. I looked around and noticed that this motherfucker had placed me in the psychiatric ward. The fucking room was padded, and the door was locked.

I bent over in pain. I was in labor, and it was confirmed when my water broke. It must have been God who sent the GYN doctor to see me just in time. Thirty minutes later, I gave birth naturally to two beautiful girls that I named Miracle and Destiny. I cried as I looked at my beautiful daughters that looked like their father, who didn't get the chance to share the moment with me. I had no one. I had to deliver my babies on the looney floor just because Dr. Kaufman was scared that I was going to report his ass. He had me admitted as some crazy bitch named Stephanie Harris, a delusional schizophrenic. Most likely they were going to take my babies from me, and that's when I knew I had to get out of that damn place.

The next morning, when the GYN that Dr. Kaufman assigned to me came to see me, I took my chances and told him the story from beginning to end. He believed me. He helped me get out with my baby girls. Once I got out, I threatened to report Dr. Kaufman and his brother if he didn't help me with my plan to get Amari back.

Everything was going according to plan, until this bitch Kelsey was left for dead.

MEEKA

If Candy thought she was going to play me like a fucking fiddle, that bitch didn't know how wrong she was. I was not one for games when it came to my fucking heart. If she thought she was about to add to the dents that were already there, she had another think coming.

I left her house and slammed the door behind me. I was pissed off, but I had a trick for that ass. I decided to call Lexi, since I'd been missing in action. The phone rang a few times before going to voice mail, so I decided to leave a message, telling her to call me when she could.

Lexi was my only friend. She was always there for me when these females did me dirty. This time would be no different. I wasn't going to cry about being on the wrong side of a love song. I was always hooking up with women who wanted to use me or abuse me, and I was so sick and tired. I thought men weren't shit; now I believed females were no better.

I got home and stripped out of my clothes. I smelled like vomit and Chef Boyardee. Miracle and Destiny were a handful. I loved kids, but those were two kids that I was not going to miss.

As I was getting out of the shower, I heard my phone ringing, and I rushed to answer it. I was praying it wasn't Candy's crazy ass. I was so done with her. It wasn't her. It was Lexi returning my call.

"Hey, girl. What's up? How you been?" I said.

"I know your ass not going to act like you weren't missing in action and not returning my calls. I was so worried about you."

"Don't get all bent out of shape. You know this is how I do when I'm laid up."

"Yeah, but I didn't have a crazy woman after me, and since you kicked her ass, I thought she got to you," Lexi said.

"Please, Lexi, that bitch isn't that crazy."

"She's more than crazy. That bitch is insane. She shot Amari's dad and burned down Amari's house. He and his daughters have been staying with me. So while all of this was going on and you weren't returning my calls, I thought she hurt you too."

"Oh my God. What's up with this bitch? This is some new fatal attraction shit!" I said.

"That's not the half. I think she was following Amari. When he went by his dad's house to clean up the blood and clean things that got thrown around, the bitch showed up and walked in like she owned the fucking place."

"Say word."

I sat in silence as Lexi filled me in on everything that had happened. She told me how Kelsey tried to kill Amari's father and how Amari thought he had killed Kelsey.

"Lexi, this shit is unbelievable." I couldn't believe Kelsey was that crazy.

"Well, then I guess you won't believe what happened next."

"Please don't tell me it's more, Lexi?"

"Just listen," she said. "I leave work, and I just felt like someone was watching me, but as I look around, no one was there. I rushed to the car, and when I get there, a note is posted on my windshield with a picture of two little girls. So I'm stuck on why would someone leave the picture? Anyway, long story short—"

"This story is far from short," I said, interrupting her.

"Shut up, Meeka, and let me finish. Now, like I was saying before I was rudely interrupted, I get home and Amari shows me the exact picture of the same little girls. Someone handed it to Imani and told her to give it to her mom. Crazy, right?"

"And you have no idea who the kids are?"

"No, at first we thought they were a picture of Amari's twins when they were small, but he said they're not his girls. So we don't know what the fuck is going on."

"Damn, and I thought I had problems with this bitch Candy that I met. Anyway, did you guys at least report it?" I asked.

"Amari has been speaking to the detective that's on the case. It seems Kelsey gave a fake address at work. She was nowhere to be found before the incident with Amari. So now we have no clue if she's dead or alive, and if alive, who helped her ass at Amari's dad's place."

"Girl, I feel for you. Whether she's dead or alive, you know I got your back."

"I know, girl, and Mom gave me a gun for protection."

"I love your mom. She's gangsta," I said, laughing out loud.

"Whatever, girl. Let me get back to work. Amari is picking me up, and I want to be done with my work so he doesn't have to wait."

"Cool. Talk to you later."

After I hung up with my girl, I really felt bad that she was dealing with this. She'd been through so much already. She finally had a man she adored, but she had to put up with bullshit. Not blaming him, but bitches can be so thirsty.

My phone was ringing again. I had left the phone downstairs when I finished talking to Lexi so that I could finish getting dressed. I ran down to get it, even though I didn't want to. By the time I got downstairs, I had missed the call from Candy. It would have been missed anyway, because I had nothing to say to her. She probably wanted me to come watch those brats again while she ran the streets doing God knows what.

AMARI

I got a call from my aunt, telling me that my dad was awake. I was pushing eighty miles per hour in a residential area. I didn't care. I needed to get to the hospital. I had to let the school know that I had an emergency, so I was leaving. I had been posted up since nine that morning after dropping Lexi off to work. I hadn't seen anything, so I was sure they would be all right, especially since everyone at the school had been put on alert by the detective.

I rushed to my dad's room. That feeling of being blessed and having my prayers answered was overwhelming. I broke down and ran toward my dad like I was a little two-year-old. I smothered him with my hugs and kisses. My aunt and cousin were laughing at me, but I didn't care. My dad was awake.

Unlike when Kindrah was in a coma and she woke up able to speak, my dad wasn't able. The doctor said that he had also suffered a stroke, which caused his motor skills to be off.

I was just happy that he was alive and wasn't taken away from us. I called Lexi to let her know that my dad was awake and I was at the hospital. I also let her know that the girls were fine. Being the beautiful person that she was, she told me not to worry; she would have Meeka pick her and the girls up and take them home. I was blessed to have found love again; it really felt good.

My dad began dozing off, so my aunt and cousin left. I decided to stay until visiting hours were over, hoping he would wake up before it was time for me to go, but he didn't. The nurse said the meds helps him rest, as well as helping with the pain. I wanted to say, "He just woke up." I didn't need him resting; I wanted to talk to my dad.

I kissed my dad on his forehead as he had done to me so many times as a child. I walked out, wiping away my tears. I thanked God for bringing him back. I called my aunt to let her know he was sleeping and I was leaving. I told her about the detectives coming by, but the nurse told them that Dad was in no condition to answer any questions yet. I let her know that I would be back to the hospital after dropping off Lexi and the girls in the morning.

I put in for family leave at my job because my dad was going to need me. I didn't want to burden my aunt with too much, even though I knew she was going to insist on caring for her brother. I would just make sure to be there to help her.

I had the locksmith change all of my dad's locks and set up an alarm system. When he was released, I wanted him safe until they caught up with Kelsey's crazy ass.

When I got home, I was tired. Lexi already had the girls fed, bathed, and in bed. She was in the living room talking with Meeka. I said hello, kissed my baby on the lips, and went to take a much-needed shower. Lexi made her way upstairs about an hour later, telling me about Meeka's jacked-up love life that I really didn't want to hear about. Shit, my father was awake, and since I was feeling a little better, I was ready to get busy between the sheets. Lexi just kept going on and on, so I listened until she went to shower. I tried to wait on her, but I dozed off.

I had to hit her off in the shower the next morning because she was clearly upset that I had fallen asleep. I told her ass it was her fault, talking about Meeka's ass for almost two hours. When she left the bathroom, her ass had a permanent smile on her face. Yeah, I did that.

After driving the girls to school and dropping Lexi off, I headed straight to the hospital. Just like I knew she would be, my aunt was already there, cleaning up and rearranging the flowers. It looked like she had gone shopping.

"Hey, Auntie, what's in the bags?"

"I got my brother some pajamas. No one needs to see his ass hanging out with those cheap gowns that don't button or zip up. See, they only have those shoestring straps to hold it together. I got him a sheet set and pillowcase for his bed, too."

"Auntie, this is the hospital. Everything has to be sterile. You can use those things when he goes to the rehabilitation center," I said.

"I know you're not trying to say these dingy sheets on this bed are sterile. That goddamn gown with bullet holes is sterile? Child, go ahead with that bullshit. My brother's taking that shit off today."

My aunt had me and my cousin cracking up. He asked me why I got her started, because she was not going to let it end. After I agreed with Auntie, she calmed down a little. She gave my dad a sponge bath, changed his pajamas, and had us help her change the sheets with him still in the bed. My aunt had skills. She was a retired home health aide and was still good at what she knew. She said she was going to be my dad's caretaker until he got back on his feet.

I left the hospital around noon. I had to go run some errands for my dad's job and pay some bills for him. Lexi's mom was taking the girls that weekend, so it would just be me and Lexi. We hadn't decided what we were going to do yet. All had been quiet. Too quiet. You know the saying, the calm before the storm. I was hoping it didn't apply in this case. If Kelsey had any brains, she would have gotten out of town. If not, I was just hoping she left me and my family alone.

Lexi called and asked if it was okay if we had a few people over on Saturday. I told her I didn't mind. I didn't really have too many friends, so it would mostly be her friends. I'd hit up two dudes I was cool with at work and a few of my male cousins. This would be good for Lexi and me to unwind a little with some grown folks, music, and laughter.

LEXI

I was up early that morning. I was meeting Meeka at the grocery store to get what I needed for the get-together that night. Amari was still in the bed when I left. I just hoped he didn't think he was sleeping in. I needed him to make the shrimp pasta and the guacamole bowl that he was good at making. I loved it, so I knew everyone else would love it, too. I wanted him to make the lemon pepper wings and the hot wings, but Meeka was going to make them. She was a hell of a cook, too. This wasn't a dinner, so I was making sure I had all types of sides that go with drinking. I was making barbecue wings, fried chicken, and three homemade dips. I ordered mozzarella sticks, a vegetable platter, and a banging-ass order of macaroni salad from my favorite restaurant, because they made it best.

Meeka got what she needed, and she went her way. I drove to the liquor store to get some wine. I knew Amari had some issues with alcohol, so I wasn't buying any hard liquor. I told everyone to bring their own brown bag. My boo and I were only sipping on this wine. Knowing Amari, he wasn't going to touch the stuff. He would be in the backyard with his herbal medicine.

When I got back to the house, I was surprised to see Amari up and making his way around the kitchen. His eyes looked as if he had made his trip to the backyard already. All I could do was laugh at how silly he was looking.

"What's so funny?" he asked.

"You Mr. Amari. Your ass was in the backyard, wasn't you?"

"Babe, I cook better when my mind's right. You know that, because I cooked a few times in the bedroom after a visit to the backyard."

"Yeah, babe, you puts it down," I said as I hit him on the ass and kept it moving to put my groceries away.

Our little get-together was in full effect, and we were having a good time. We started up a spades game. Amari and I were dominating until his cousin, Rah, and Meeka beat us. Rah kept trying to get Meeka's digits. I wanted to tell him so bad that he was barking up the wrong tree, but it wasn't my place. We had good food, great music, and I was feeling nice off of three glasses of Moscato. My babe was enjoying himself as he watched me dancing. I tried to get him to come and dance with me. At first he declined, until he saw one of his coworkers dancing with me.

"Jealous, are we?" I asked.

"Not at all. My baby asked me to dance, so here I am. Let's dance."

Meeka played "I Want to Be Your Man" by Roger. My baby and I danced like there was no one else in the room. I loved this song, and what better song to dance to with the man that I was in love with? All the couples in attendance were now on the floor, dancing with their significant others. I looked to my left, and Meeka was dancing with Rah. Was my girl switching teams? I smiled at her, and she smiled back and rolled her eyes as if to say it was just a dance.

This get-together was needed. I felt normal again. Looking over my shoulder every day had me stressed the hell out. This felt good. I was really enjoying myself.

The party started winding down. Everyone was leaving. Meeka stayed back to help me clean. Rah wanted to stay back to offer Meeka a ride home, and I didn't want Meeka to hurt his feelings, because she would have. I had Amari tell him that Meeka was staying the night.

Amari was in the kitchen emptying cups, beer bottles, and putting away food that was left over. As Meeka and I were cleaning the living room, someone rang the doorbell. I thought that Rah had come back, and I opened the door without looking out the peephole. It was a female who looked vaguely familiar.

"How can I help you?" I asked.

"For starters, you can step to the side and let me in."

"Excuse you. Who the hell are you?"

I heard Meeka come from behind me to see who was standing there being rude.

"Candy, what the fuck are you doing here? What part of 'I don't want anything to do with you' don't you understand?" Meeka asked.

"Sweetie, don't flatter yourself. I'm not into women. I just needed your stupid ass to give me the information I needed on your little friend here."

"Candy, what the hell are you talking about?"

Next thing I knew, Kelsey and some tall African man were now on the scene, and that was when I started to panic. I wanted to scream for Amari or run to get the gun my mom had given me, but shock kept me from moving.

"K, I always knew you were soft. You have the heart of a bitch," Candy said to the tall man.

My eyes grew big as she pulled out a gun and shot him right in front of all of us. Meeka and I ran back inside. Kelsey backed in with her hands up, as Candy was now holding her at gunpoint. We were all in the living room. I was wondering where the hell Amari was. Granted she had a silencer on the gun, but he had to have heard all the arguing, unless he was in the backyard smoking again. I prayed that he came and saved us from whatever was unfolding, because these bitches were crazy.

"So, Kelsey, you have nothing to say now? What's wrong? Does the cat have your tongue? Did you forget that I told you to stay away from my man?" Candy yelled.

Kelsey just stood there like she had seen a ghost. As crazy as her ass was, she was frightened just like the rest of us.

We all heard Amari as he closed the back door, unaware of what he was about to walk in on. When he entered the living room, he looked from Kelsey to Candy, and he, too, looked like he had seen a ghost.

Candy stared at Amari with tears in her eyes as she spoke. "Amari?" she stuttered.

"Kindrah?" He squinted his eyes as if he wasn't seeing clearly.

"Kindrah? What the fuck? I thought she was dead. Would someone like to tell me what's going on here?" I yelled.

I guess Kelsey seeing Amari gave her the battery she needed in her back, as she was brave all of a sudden.

"Let me do the honors," Kelsey said. "This is Kindrah, who I killed—well, who is supposed to be dead. She came and destroyed my life with Amari. I got rid of her and built my life with him again, only to have your ass do the same," she said as she reached in her jacket pocket, pulling out her gun and pointing it at me.

Kelsey's gun was on me, and Amari's supposed-to-be-dead girlfriend's gun was still pointed at Kelsey. Amari stood frozen, like he was conflicted. Kindrah started crying but continued to point her gun at Kelsey.

"Amari, you know I would never leave you willingly. During surgery, I slipped into a coma, and Dr. Kaufman decided he would fake my death. Remember, he was the doctor from my first accident. According to him, he believed that someone was trying to kill me, so he was trying to protect me.

"When I woke up from the coma eight months later, I was pregnant with your twins and being held against my will. I was hurt and alone. When I told Dr. Kaufman I was going to report him, he had me admitted on the psychiatric ward. I had to deliver your babies on a fucking psych ward floor, all by myself.

"I went through so much to make it back to you, but it took time. Once I was back, it was brought to my attention that this bitch was trying to destroy you. I was going to deal with her first before coming back to you, but it didn't work out that way. I'm sorry for everything. Please believe that everything I've ever done was for you," Kindrah said.

"Stop the crying, bitch," Kelsey said. "All he wanted with your ass was the friendship that meant the world to him. As soon as you saw that he was falling for me, that's when you filled his head with nonsense, so you had to go."

"Well, bitch, I'm still here. I have his daughters, and we're going to be a family," Kindrah said.

As I stood listening to these two delusional bitches, I wasn't even scared anymore. I was becoming angry that these two bitches were standing in my living room arguing over a man who didn't want either one of them. Kelsey, he had never wanted, and this Kindrah person, he had grieved for and moved on.

As Kelsey continued to argue with Kindrah, I caught her off guard with a punch to her temple that dropped that bitch to the floor. Her gun fell from her hand. I went for it but froze when Kindrah cocked the gun to pull the trigger.

Amari screamed, "Kindrah, noooo!" The gun went off, but his screaming startled her, and her aim was off as the bullet hit the mirror on the wall.

KINDRAH

If I didn't see it with my own eyes, I wouldn't have believed it. Amari was in love with someone else. His eyes said it all, and the panic in his voice as I pulled the trigger broke my heart. If Amari died, I would have never loved another man like I loved him. Before my accident, I believed the same of him, but that wasn't the case. He was in love with a woman that wasn't me. The tears and the broken pieces of my heart clouded my vision as I now pointed the gun at Amari.

"Amari, how could you? I loved you with my all. I believed you felt the same way about me. How could you give your heart that belonged to me to someone else?"

"Kindrah, put the gun down so we can talk about this. Please, before someone gets hurt," he said.

LEXI

I saw Meeka pick up the gun off the floor as Kindrah and Amari were talking. I mean, the dick was good and he was a wonderful man, but these bitches were crazy, talking about killing for him. If I made it out of this, I was going to need some counseling.

I assumed Kindrah was the one that had been following me and the one who left the picture of the babies. I was really in a state of shock as I was knocked out of my daydream, hearing Kindrah say, "Amari, I love you. Without you, I don't want to live. If I can't have you, no one can."

As she raised the gun to shoot Amari, Meeka pulled the trigger, hitting Kindrah twice. Amari ran over to Kindrah, who hit the floor.

I was conflicted as Amari held her, crying and yelling for us to call an ambulance. Meeka called 911 as I stood in place, unable to watch the scene before me, but at the same time, unable not to watch. It tugged at my heart to see him crying over a woman who had just tried to kill him. I had to remind myself that they had a history, but did it make me feel any better? Not at all. I didn't even know how to explain this crazy scene to the police. The only good thing about the whole scene was that since the whole Kelsey business had started, we installed cameras for safety. I would be turning over the tapes.

As the paramedics arrived and began working on Kindrah, Amari pulled me to the side and told me not to mention the tapes. I was taken back, but when I heard him tell the police officers that Kelsey shot and killed the African man and shot Kindrah, I felt lightheaded. Why was he protecting her? She was going to kill me and kill his ass, too. Meeka wasn't speaking at all. I think she was in shock. Kelsey wasn't dead;

she was just knocked unconscious. She was going to jail for murder and attempted murder, not to mention the crime that she had committed against Amari's dad once he was able to implicate her in that case.

Kindrah was asking for Amari. Her ass was shot twice in the shoulder, not life threatening. Why the fuck was she asking for my man? Amari told the police officer that he would go down to the police station to give his written statement the next day.

Once the officers left, Amari said he needed to go to where Kindrah was staying because she had left the babies there alone, and he had to go if, in fact, the kids were his. I was floored. Why wouldn't he just send the officers to the residence? My best friend was sitting there in shock. I was still upset about this whole ordeal, and he was worried about kids that may not even be his.

AMARI

I could see the hurt in Lexi's eyes. She had to understand that the woman who I loved and had been friends with wasn't dead. She was standing in my living room. Yes, she had just tried to kill me, but I thought I understood why. I was still in shock.

Lexi was upset because I left to go see if the children really existed. I hoped she understood my position as a man. I would have asked her to go with me, but she had to tend to Meeka.

Once I pulled up to the house, I started to get nervous. If there were really kids inside, were they okay? Who was to say how long she had left them here alone?

I turned the knob, and the door opened. I walked upstairs, checking every room until I found theirs. They were both sleeping in separate cribs. I looked around until I found car seats. I went to the kitchen to find bottles and milk, and I saw some jars of baby food on the counter, so I packed them, too. I didn't know how Lexi was going to feel about me bringing them back to the house, but I was going to soon find out.

I had a killer headache. I had absorbed so much that night that I felt as if my head was going to burst. I wished my dad was able to give me the much-needed advice that he always gave me.

When I got back to Lexi's place, the news vans were in front of the house and the reporter was reporting. I hoped Lexi had called her mom, because the story was definitely making the morning news.

When I walked in carrying the two car seats, the look on Lexi's face said it all. I placed them on the couch in the living room and wrapped my arms around her as she cried in my arms. No words were spoken as I held her. I wanted her to know that I would never abandon her on purpose. Meeka was in the guest room, so Lexi told me to put Kindrah's girls to bed in the room our girls shared.

The next morning, the calls didn't stop. Everyone saw the news and wanted to know what had happened. I still didn't know the full story. Lexi's mom came over without the girls. She didn't want to expose them to the scene that was taking place in front of the house. She was asking question after question, and we were trying our best to answer them, when she heard the babies cry. I left the room for Lexi to explain, because I didn't know where to begin. This story was so unbelievable.

I didn't even have time to think of how I felt about Kindrah being alive and claiming to have given birth to my daughters. I did know I needed to get to the hospital. I needed some answers, but who was going to keep her daughters? Lexi had been through so much that I wouldn't dare ask her.

I dropped the girls off to Rah and his mother so I could go see Kindrah. I still needed to go by the police station, and I had forgotten I also had to visit my dad.

When I walked into Kindrah's hospital room, all kinds of emotions were going through my body. I honestly didn't know which ones to run on. Here, lying in a hospital bed, was my best friend, my lover, who I had thought was dead. How could I not feel something? I still loved her. I never stopped loving her, so how could I just turn off those feelings?

She was quiet as I just stood staring at her, still not believing she was there in the flesh. I wanted to touch her, hold her, and never let her go, but what about Lexi? She was my new love.

"So you're going to just stand there looking at me like I have two heads?" she asked.

"You have to give me a minute. This is hard. I can't believe you're here. I was at the funeral. I watched your body be lowered into the ground. I mourned for you. My world was flipped upside down because it hurt me so bad that you were gone."

"So why was it so easy for you to move on?"

"Believe me when I tell you it wasn't easy. It took me a very long time to look at another woman in that way," I answered.

"Do you love her?"

Why was it taking me so long to answer the question? I knew that I loved Lexi. I was in love with her, so where did that warm feeling go that I always got when thinking of her? It was gone. How was that possible? I was so confused. Were my feelings not real? Or was it that Kindrah was clouding my mind with her intense stare?

"Kindrah, I'm not here to talk about Lexi. I need to know what in the hell happened to you. I get the part you spoke about at Lexi's house, but once you were free, why didn't you go to the police and tell your story so that you could come back home to me and the girls? You just watched from afar and allowed me to fall in love, thinking you were gone." I was getting angry. I had just admitted that I fell in love. She would have to own up for some of the reason I moved on. Had I known she was alive, I would have never pursued anyone else.

"Amari, when I was freed with the help of Dr. K, I came— me and both your daughters. As I pulled up, I saw you, the girls, and Kelsey leaving together very early in the morning. I was pissed. I couldn't believe you went back to her crazy ass. It was like every time I wanted to see you, she was always there. I felt I did what I needed to do to get rid of her to get you back. Then the tables turned, and she was out, but some random chick was in the picture. Amari, you know that out of every piece of me, you've always been the best. I would never leave you. I loved you then, and I love you now."

I watched as she cried. My heartstrings were being pulled as I walked over to her and held her. I couldn't believe I was holding her in my arms. We were both crying by now. I was really doing a lot of crying lately. I had to man up. Love will have you acting like a bitch.

It was going on 6:00 p.m. when my phone alerted me I had a text message.

Lexi: Amari, where are you? The detective just called and said he couldn't reach you. He said you never showed up to the police station. Call me.

Oh, shit. I had forgotten all about the detective, my father, and Kindrah's daughters that I left with my cousin. I knew in my heart that they were my daughters. They looked like Kindrah and me. She finally told me she had named them Miracle and Destiny, because it was a miracle they survived, and it was destined that we would be a family again. I didn't want to leave her, but I had to. I also had to remember I had Tiara and Tiana to tend to as well. I really needed my herbal medicine. I had no idea what I was going to do.

"You have to go, don't you?" she asked.

"I'll be back tomorrow. I have to pick up my girls and your girls."

"Amari, my girls are your girls too."

"I know. I'm sorry. This has been a hell of a roller coaster ride these last two days. My mind is all over the place right now."

"I understand. Kiss all the girls for me, and I will see you tomorrow."

I reached over to give her a hug. It seemed natural as my lips touched hers and we kissed. It felt like we had never parted. My love for her was the same, as my body got that familiar feeling that only Kindrah gave it. I had to break the kiss. I would have been taking her clothes off if I didn't stop. I missed all of her.

I texted Lexi back once I was in my car.

Amari: I'm on my way now. I was at the hospital with my dad when the detective called. His call went straight to voice mail because I didn't have a signal.

Lexi: Okay, see you when you get home. The girls are home. Love you.

Amari: Okay, see you guys soon.

LEXI

I tried to convince myself that Kindrah being alive wouldn't interfere with what Amari and I had, but now I was not so sure. Something had changed. He didn't feel like my Amari anymore. I had been crying almost every day these past few weeks, because he had been so distant. I felt my heart breaking all over again as I sat at work, staring at the letter he had given me that morning. My Amari never had a problem communicating with me and would have never left me a letter. We'd always been up front with each other. My hands shook as I removed the letter from the envelope.

Hey Lexi,
I know you're probably wondering why I'm writing you a letter when I see you every day and night. Truth is, I couldn't look you in your face and tell you what I needed to tell you, so yes, I took the punk route and decided to write you this letter. As you know, the DNA results for Miracle and Destiny came back 99.9% that I'm the father. I know you said that you would have no problem with it, being they were conceived before we met, but I wouldn't be a man to continue living with you knowing that my heart belongs to someone else. I gave you a piece of my heart in default. I didn't know Kindrah was still alive. She has my heart in its entirety, and with her and my children is where I need to be. I never set out to hurt you, and I hope that you forgive me.
Amari

I held onto my stomach as I ran to the bathroom and released that morning's breakfast. How could he do this to me? No discussion, a fucking letter, a bullshit letter at that.
Why, Amari? You knew what I went through with Imani's dad.

I felt sick to my stomach. I had to leave work. No way would I be able to get anything done. My heart had been broken.

When I got home, Amari's car was in the driveway. I walked in, and all of his things and the girls' things were sitting near the front door. He must have been moving out while I was at work. It really hurt that he was going to just bounce without saying good-bye.

When he came downstairs, carrying his laptop and a few other things and saw me, shock and guilt were written all over his face.

"So you were just going to leave and not say good-bye? I thought we were better than that," I said.

"I just figured it would be easier this way."

"Amari, none of this is easy. My heart hurts, and I'm confused. I don't understand why you're leaving me. So you just stop loving me overnight?"

"I didn't stop loving you, Lexi. It's really hard to explain."

"Amari, you need to explain, because I need help understanding how you can just walk away. What we had was real."

He walked over and sat on the couch. I followed him, trying hard not to cry, looking at the man I loved, who I wasn't going to see again once he walked out the door.

"Lexi, you knew how I felt about Kindrah. It wasn't a secret. Had she not been forced to fake her death, I would have still been with her. I missed the birth of my twins, and I missed out on continuing to love her and make her my wife. Will things between Kindrah and me pick up where they left off? I don't know, but I'm willing to take that chance."

"So what about me and Imani? You do remember Imani, who has grown to love you and the girls?" I asked.

"I love her too, and that's why this is so hard for me. But I will regret it if I don't try and get my life back with Kindrah and my daughters."

"Amari, she isn't stable. She's no different than Kelsey, and you're going to trust her around your girls?"

"Lexi, don't do that. I have known Kindrah from childhood. Yes, I trust her. The night you met her, she was acting on emotions. She's not like that."

"So let me ask you a question. Do you love me? And are you still in love with me?"

"Lexi, I love you, and yes, I'm in love with you, but like I said in my letter, Kindrah has my heart as a whole."

"Wow, this really hurts me. Just let me say that I never begged a man to stay when he didn't want to, and I'm not going to start now. I do want you to take this. We can discuss this at another time, because right now, I'm mentally and physically drained." As I handed him the results from my doctor's appointment the week before, I asked him to close the door on his way out and to leave the keys on the coffee table.

Once I reached my room, all that I held in was released, and I cried until I wasn't able to produce another tear.

AMARI

I sat staring at the positive test results of Lexi's pregnancy test and couldn't move. What the fuck was my ass going to do now? I heard Lexi upstairs crying, so I went up, got in bed, and held her until it was time for the girls to be picked up from school. No words were spoken as she got in her car and I got in mine, as we both were headed in the same direction and destination.

I let her go ahead of me to pick up Imani, waiting until she left before I got out of the car to pick up my girls. I'd decided to take the girls to the rehab to see their grandpa. He was doing much better. He was able to speak a little better but still slurred his words. He was also able to hold the pen and write what he wasn't able to say. He would be home in no time. The doctor said he was progressing well.

When I told my dad Kelsey was being charged for the crime against him, he showed no emotions about the situation. When I told him Kindrah was alive, I had to relive the whole story, because he wanted to hear it. He grabbed the pad and asked me about Lexi. I told him all that was going on, and his response on the pad was, *And I thought I had it bad*. We both laughed, even though it wasn't a laughing matter.

I stayed with my dad for as long as I could. I was confused as to whose place I was going to. I never took my things from Lexi's house that day. I just couldn't find it in my heart to do it.

I got the girls ready to leave, and I placed them in their cars seats. As I walked around to get in the driver's seat, I noticed an envelope with my name on it taped to my window. I sat in the car to read the letter. I had just given Lexi a letter, but I wasn't big on receiving them.

Dear Amari,

I can't believe that I'm writing this letter. I waited so long to be a part of your life again. I have to admit that I have been selfish and was putting my needs before anyone else's, but becoming a mom and watching you interact with the girls these past few days did something to me. I realized that the love that Tiara and Tiana have in their eyes when you walk into the room shows me how much they love and adore you. I want my girls to love and adore me in that same manner. In order for them to love, adore, and respect me as their mother, I have to become a better person.

Amari, what I'm about to tell you is not to hurt you. I hope that you find it in your heart to forgive me and try to understand. I'm not going to go into any details, but I killed Tanisha and her parents. I'm telling you this to tell you that I'm not that person anymore. Last night, I thought long and hard, and I want to become a better person for my girls. I want them to grow up and become beautiful little girls, just like Tiara and Tiana, and right now, I can't offer them that.

Amari, it's too late for me. The Kindrah you fell in love with is no more, and there is no coming back from what I did. I'm a murderer who almost made the mistake of taking your life, and I'm sorry.

I saw how you looked at Lexi. You love her, and she loves you. She genuinely loves you the same way I used to love you before I let jealousy and hate dictate who I became. All I ask is you please try to forgive me and raise our daughters. Let them know that I loved them with my all, and my leaving them is to give them better.

If you decide to give this letter to the authorities, I understand, but it will be too late. By the time they find me, I will already be gone. I love you, Mr. Amari James. I would say I'll see you on the other side, but I doubt we will end up in the same place.

Love you. Please take care of my girls, Amari, and give all of them a kiss for me.

P.S. The girls are at the house. Everything you need is in the suitcase I left on the couch.

Kindrah

***

I sat still for at least twenty minutes, trying to digest the letter with tears that wouldn't stop falling. I almost forgot the girls were in the car with me as my body heaved up and down. The pain was too much. She had just come back into my life, and I didn't want to lose her again.

I managed to text Lexi. I asked her to come to the rehab center to pick up Tiara and Tiana. I made sure to text her the address and my dad's room number because she hadn't been there before. I kissed my babies as I brought them back up to my father's room and told my dad that Lexi was on her way to get them.

I rushed out of his room to get to Miracle and Destiny, praying that they were okay and unharmed.

LEXI

When I got to the address that Amari had given me, I ran to room 313, thinking that something was wrong because Amari wasn't answering his phone. When I walked in, Tiara ran to me and said, "Dada cry." Now I was really nervous.

"Edward, do you know where Amari is?"

He grabbed the note pad and wrote, *He dropped the girls off, kissed them, and ran out.*

I tried his phone at least ten more times before I got frustrated. I took the girls and left. I sat at home on pins and needles, praying nothing happened to him. I didn't trust Kindrah.

After Meeka left to go home, I did what I needed to do for the girls. I sat down and poured me a glass of Moscato, trying to calm my nerves. Amari walked in with Miracle and Destiny at about 10:00 p.m. His eyes were bloodshot red, and he looked like he had aged.

"Babe, what happened?"

"Can you put the girls down in the guest room so we can talk?"

He sounded so defeated. I took the girls upstairs, changed both girls' diapers, and put them in clean undershirts. I pulled out Imani's old playpen, placed a blanket inside, and put them down with a warm bottle.

When I got back downstairs, Amari was pouring a drink. That's when I knew the shit was serious. I thought about stopping him, but since it was only wine, I left him alone. He walked into the den, and I followed him.

"Amari, what's going on that's causing you to drink?"

He handed me an envelope. I pulled out the letter and started reading it. I was at a loss for words. As I tried to find some comforting words to offer him, I came up empty. I'd met and seen crazy before, but the shit these bitches were doing over some dick was insane. I loved Amari, but I would never go to that extreme to keep him. Shit, he broke up with me, and yes, I was hurt, but I'd be damned if I was going to take Kindrah out. Hell, no. I love me more.

"Amari, did you go to the police?" I asked.

"Yes. They told me she had to be missing for at least twenty-four hours."

"Even after you showed them the letter, Amari? I find that hard to believe."

"I didn't show them the letter. She indicated that she committed murder in the letter. How would I explain to my daughters that their mother was in jail for murder if the police found her? She asked me to protect them, and that's what I'm going to do."

My heart hurt for Amari, but he was starting to blow mine over his precious Kindrah. He was on his fifth drink when I decided to stop him. I didn't want him to lean on the bottle for comfort. That's what I was there for.

"Amari, let's keep the faith that Kindrah is okay. I need for you to come upstairs and get some rest. We can try to figure this out tomorrow."

It took him three more drinks to finally agree to get some rest as he staggered up the stairs. He passed out as soon as his head hit the pillow. I removed his boots and covered him up.

I was getting the girls ready when the morning news caught my attention.

"Some of you may remember the story I reported last week that involved Kelsey Reed, who was arrested for the murder of Dr. Kaufman and the attempted murder of Kindrah Watts—the same Kindrah Watts who supposedly died almost two years ago from injuries from a car accident, but was found at the scene very much alive and suffering from a gunshot wound to her shoulder.

"It has been reported that Dr. Kaufman faked her death while she was in a coma, stating he did it for her safety as he feared someone was trying to kill her. That case is under investigation.

"Today, I'm sorry to report that the body of Kindrah Watts was found at about six o'clock this morning in her car. She was parked in front of Roosevelt Park with a single gunshot wound to the head. It appears to be a case of suicide.

"Tune in at five o'clock for more on this story."

I stood with my hand over my mouth. How was I going to tell Amari this without destroying him?

It turned out that I didn't have to. He was standing behind me with Miracle in his arms, staring at the television in disbelief.

MEEKA

I sat watching the news with a smile on my face. When Lexi had called me to sit with the kids, I already knew what was going on. It was music to my ears that Kindrah's death was being ruled a suicide. I told that bitch not to fuck with my heart. I told her what I'd been through, but did she care? No, she didn't, so she got dealt with.

I caught that bitch slipping as I held the gun to Miracle's head. I told that bitch if she had any last words to Amari, she needed to write them down, because she wouldn't live to say them to him. I didn't care what she wrote, but she needed to start writing, so I kept the gun to her baby's head until she was done.

I carried her ugly-ass kids upstairs and put them in their cribs. I sat down at the table with her as I read the letter. I wasn't a dumb bitch. Her ass could have been telling his ass about me. When I finished reading her letter, I was in a state of shock. I was glad I got at her ass before she got at me. This bitch was certifiable.

I had the bitch put the letter in an envelope and give it to me. I put it in my pocket. I wasn't worried about prints because I wore gloves. I had that bitch drive to Roosevelt Park.

I put the gun in her hand and told the bitch if she didn't pull the trigger, her babies would be dead by morning. Her last words were to please make sure Amari got her letter. So after that bitch shot herself in the head, I made sure she was dead.

Thanks to Amari's pussy-sniffing cousin, Rah, I knew where to find Amari. I granted Kindrah's last wish and taped the envelope to Amari's window on the driver's side of his car. For Rah's good deed, maybe I would switch teams for a day to give him a little taste. His ass was a cutie.

AMARI

Lexi and I were now raising five kids as our own, and we had one on the way. Amari Jr. was due in just a few more weeks. This had been a rough journey.

I was blessed to say that my dad made a full recovery. The support of him and my aunt had really helped us a lot. At first I thought I was going to lose my mind, but once everyone pitched in and gave us a hand, it got much easier. Lexi's mom took the girls faithfully every weekend to give Lexi and I time to do things that needed to be done for my li'l man's arrival.

I was in another funk for a while, but Lexi kept the bottle away from me. She was there every step of the way to pull me back up when I was falling. I was glad she stuck with me through it all. Even when I was going to leave her, she stayed. That's why last month, she became Mrs. Lexi James, wife of Amari James.

AMARI

Two Months Later

I sat watching my wife sleep. I loved the way her tongue hung slightly out of her mouth, resting on her bottom lip. She was beautiful. Even sleeping, her beauty couldn't be denied. That was my heart lying in that bed. She had been my ride or die, and it hurt me to know that I had to share with her something I had planned on taking to my grave. We were in marital bliss, and this news could ruin it all.

We had finally gone on our honeymoon. We both wanted to wait until the baby was born, so we waited until Amari Jr. turned a month old and we were comfortable enough to leave him and the girls with her mom. After all that had happened we were leery, but her mom and my dad assured us that the kids would be fine.

We had just returned from our beautiful honeymoon in Antigua just for me to come home to bullshit in my fucking mailbox. It was a good thing that Lexi had to use the bathroom, because she would have been the one taking the mail out of the box. She had been drinking on the plane ride home, and she had gone to the bathroom twice on the plane and once again before we left the airport. She was not a drinker, so I was puzzled as to why she was drinking so much. I asked her if something was bothering her, but she insisted that she was fine. If she didn't have to use the bathroom, she would have been pulling this bullshit out of the mailbox.

I had no doubt that she loved me, but that still didn't stop me from thinking the worst. She stood with me through it all, but everyone has a breaking point. Unfortunately, I thought that when she heard what I had to tell her, this would be hers.

I took the letter, put it back in the envelope, and placed it in the bottom of the bag that I kept my gym clothes in. I got back in the bed, wrapped my arms around Lexi, and fell asleep with a heavy heart.

LEXI

I sat in the kitchen sipping on my second shot of vodka. I was deep in thought as I looked out the window. I knew that I had to stop drinking and get my mind right, because we would be picking the kids up that night. All my life I had been taught right from wrong, and I had lived by the morals that my parents instilled in me. Now I sat wondering if those same morals would cost me my marriage.

I decided to focus on something else. I promised Meeka that I would upload the pictures from my honeymoon, so I poured the remaining vodka into the sink and put the glass in the dishwasher.

Amari was walking around like he had the weight of the world on his shoulders. He looked how I felt. I wanted to comfort him, but my conscience wouldn't allow me to as I proceeded up the stairs to our bedroom. Looking at the pictures from our honeymoon had me in tears as the reality of what I'd done made me realize that this could, in fact, be the end of Amari and me.

I hit the SEND button, sending all of the pictures to Meeka and putting some on my Facebook timeline.

KELSEY

I had promised Amari that I was going to turn his world upside down, and that was a promise I planned on keeping. I didn't believe in God, but I would say good looking on getting me out of my current situation, because jail wasn't a place I needed, or wanted, to be. The way they treated you in that place was ridiculous, and don't let me begin on the shit they called food. It was even more ridiculous.

I was sure that Amari had gotten my package by now. I wished I could have been a fly on the wall when he opened it, or when he shared it with the wife.

I couldn't believe he had married that bitch. Once again, he made the wrong choice, and this time, I would not stop until he was either broken or dead, whichever one came first.

When I heard that Kindrah was dead for the second time, I just knew that would push him over the edge, but it didn't. In fact, he seemed to be doing just fine. He had a wife and a new baby, and he must have been the father of Kindrah's bastard children, because I saw he had them, too.

Yes, I was still watching and waiting. I sat on the park bench, watching the children play. I watched as parents pushed their children on the swings, and I looked at the dad standing at the end of the slide with love in his eyes as he waited on his son to slide down so that he could catch him. I felt nauseated as I continued to watch. The whole scene was becoming sickening as the fear of becoming a parent began to set in.

I had found out in prison that I was pregnant during the physical they give you during intake. The first few nights, I cried because I had always wanted to be with Amari and have his child. The thought of how this baby was conceived hurt me to my core. Amari had to pay for what he did.

Or course, if he wanted to be a family once he found out I was pregnant, I would give him a pass.

AMARI

Something was bothering Lexi, and I had no idea what it was. I didn't know if she could feel that something was horribly wrong and that was why she'd been distant and drinking. I had no idea, but what I did know was that it was time for me to sit her down and be honest with her about the package I had received.

How in the hell was I going to explain to her that Kelsey was claiming to be pregnant by me? The first question she was going to ask me was how that was humanly possible when I claimed I never had any sexual contact with her. I just couldn't believe Kelsey would stop at nothing to destroy me. Even from her jail cell, she was going full force with her threats.

"Amari, we need to talk," Lexi said, interrupting my thoughts.

I took a deep breath, dreading this conversation that I wasn't really prepared for. Lexi was already sitting at the kitchen island, sipping from her favorite cup, the one the kids had given her that said *Mom* on the front.

I nervously took a seat to join her. I would have been more comfortable having this conversation anywhere but the kitchen, because of the number of sharp knives and other objects, including a pot or pan that she could bust me upside my head with. I could feel her eyes watching my every move. When I looked up to meet her stare, she looked scared, and she had tears in her eyes. I became concerned as I reached for her.

"Babe, what's wrong?" I asked, forgetting all about my worries. When she didn't answer, I tried again. "Lexi! Stop crying and talk to me," I said, regretting my tone as I watched her jump slightly.

"I'm sorry, Lexi. I didn't mean to yell at you, but you're scaring me. Just talk to me, please," I said more calmly.

"Amari, I did something that I can't take back," she said through her tears.

"Lexi, you can talk to me about anything, and you know this, so please stop crying and just tell me what you need to tell me," I said, getting slightly agitated.

"Amari, you know I love you with everything I have, and I would do anything for you. Truth is, I have been having a hard time since the day you told the officers that Kelsey shot that man."

"And why would you be having a problem with it?" I asked, really agitated now.

"Amari, I haven't been sleeping. I've even been drinking to try to block the guilt I feel every day, so I took the tape down to the district attorney's office that's handling Kelsey's case, and they assured me that someone would look at it and proceed accordingly."

"Lexi, please tell me you didn't do no stupid shit like that. After all the bullshit she put this family through, you go and try to get her released from fucking jail?" I yelled, not caring about her feelings this time.

"Amari, I was having nightmares. I just couldn't live with myself knowing I was sending an innocent woman to jail."

"Are you fucking insane? That bitch isn't a woman. She's a monster who didn't give a fuck about shooting my father and leaving him for dead. And aren't you the same person that was going to help me dispose of the body when we thought Kelsey was dead?"

"Yes, Amari. I'm that same person, but that's different. She forced your hand; you weren't trying to kill her. If you had accidentally killed her, I was riding with you because I love you. Kelsey didn't kill that man, and I just couldn't live with myself sending her to jail for something she didn't do," she cried.

"Well, Ms. I-couldn't-live-with-myself, I hope you're happy, because that same bitch you gave a fuck about don't give a fuck about you, me, or our family," I said as I put the package in front of her, walked out of the kitchen, and straight out the front door. I felt like putting my hand through a fucking wall. That's how mad I was. I left because I didn't want to do or say something that I would regret later.

LEXI

I finally stood up and walked to the door because it made no sense to sit and stare at those papers any longer. I looked out and Amari's car was gone. I needed answers, and I didn't care how upset he was with me. You didn't leave this kind of shit on a table and walk the fuck out without giving me an explanation for this foolishness. My only question was, how could this be? He told me that he never had any sexual contact with Kelsey, so his information and what she was requesting made no sense at all.

My tears had dried up, and all I felt was hurt and anger at the thought of Amari lying to me and having sexual contact with the crazy bitch that had turned our lives upside down. The part that hurt the most was him saying that she was doing all of these things and he didn't know why.

I called his phone back to back, but he kept sending me to voice mail. I sat in deep thought, thinking about what this bitch was requesting, and it made me sick to my stomach, knowing that I was the reason this bitch got released. I knew for a fact that she was no longer in prison, because you couldn't request something like this from a jail cell.

I felt so fucking stupid, and now I understood why Amari got so upset. This bitch truly belonged behind bars. According to the request she sent, it seemed that this crazy bitch went to an OB/GYN and had them take cell samples from the membranes surrounding her fetus. Now she wanted Amari to make an appointment at the same lab that the samples were sent to so they could swab the inside of his cheek, as well as hers, to perform the paternity test.

Now, I understand wanting to prove the paternity of your child to the man you claim to be the father, but why not wait until the birth of the child? Knowing this crazy chick, in her

mind, she thought that if she proved that Amari was the
father, he was going to leave his family and be with her. How
wrong she would be. Yes, he was about family, but he would
never be with her. She was tainted and crazy as hell. If, by
some crazy chance, he was the father of her child, I could see
him in court to get custody of the child, but be with that crazy
bitch? Never.

I could honestly say that if Amari decided to leave me for
helping this crazy bitch get out of jail, I wouldn't even blame
him. I couldn't help but to think about what would happen if
he decided to stay and work on our marriage and this baby
turned out to be his. Would I be able to stay? That would be
five kids in the equation that didn't belong to me.

I was really giving myself a headache, so I decided to get
up and log on to the computer because I needed to know if
Kelsey was released. I did an inmate search and sure enough,
this bitch was released. I felt like crying again, but I didn't
have time to cry. I needed to fix this.

I tried Amari a few more times, and after still getting no
answer, I grabbed my car keys and left the house. I needed to
clear my head. I swear I could have killed this bitch.

AMARI

Lexi had been blowing up my phone, but I wasn't ready to talk to her just yet. I really didn't want her to find out like this, but she had really pissed me off doing some stupid shit like this without talking to me first. It still wouldn't have changed my mind if she talked to me first, but I could have talked her out of doing something so stupid. I would have pointed out why it wouldn't have been a good idea for Kelsey's crazy ass to be on the streets. True, she didn't kill dude, but she had shot my father several times and left him for dead, so I didn't give a fuck if she rotted in that jail cell.

I hated Kelsey for everything she had done to my family, and it hurt me that Lexi didn't see it that way. I just couldn't believe that we were in this place again. We had a beautiful wedding and an amazing honeymoon just to once again be living in a fucking nightmare.

I wanted to go and talk to my dad about the situation but was tired of being a burden when it came to my problems. I knew he wouldn't mind, but at some point in my life, I needed to man up. I was going to be the man that my father raised and handle this shit on my own. I'd be damned if my family went through this heartache again. I swear I could have killed this bitch.

LEXI

When I got back to the house, I noticed Amari's car was sitting in the driveway. When I got upstairs to the bedroom, he was in bed with his back facing the door. He appeared to be sleeping, so I took this as my opportunity to get cleaned up. I went into the bathroom, took off my clothes, and put them in the hamper as I prepared my bath. I just wanted to soak away all of the stress I was feeling.

After my bath, I felt a little better. I grabbed my clothes out of the hamper, took them to the laundry room, and put them in the wash. Once back upstairs, I pulled the covers back and joined my husband in bed. Well, at least I hoped he was still my husband.

To my surprise, when I got into bed, he pulled me close to him and we cuddled. No words were spoken. I closed my eyes and said a silent prayer that we would be all right and that we would remain a family.

Eventually he was going to have to explain to me how he could possibly be Kelsey's baby's father. I also wanted him, with me of course, to go and give this crazy bitch her test so that we could prove her wrong. Something in my gut told me that he was not her baby's father.

I heard my phone ringing and then it stopped. My house phone starting ringing too, but I still wasn't going to leave Amari's arms until my cell phone starting ringing again. I figured that it had to be important, possibly my mom calling about one of the children, so I got up to answer it.

It wasn't my mom calling; it was Meeka. She was all out of breath and telling me to turn to Channel 7. I hung up the phone and grabbed the remote off of the dresser to turn on the news. I couldn't help but have a déjà vu moment as I watched.

"A woman was stabbed to death inside her home last night. Paramedics rushed to the home after being called by a neighbor who saw blood seeping from the inside of the apartment out into the hallway. The woman had numerous stab wounds to her body and neck. The victim was identified by her identification found in the home by the officers who were on the scene. It's being reported that Kelsey Reed, who was recently released from prison and cleared of all charges, is the victim in this horrible crime. No arrests have been made, and police are asking anyone who may have any information to please contact the crime unit."

"I'm confused. How was that bitch out of jail to be killed?" she asked. I hadn't even confided in Meeka when I decided to turn the tape over, because I knew she would try to talk me out of it, just like Amari would have done.

"Meeka, don't get upset and yell at me, because Amari did enough yelling of his own," I said, really not in the mood to be judged again.

"Lexi, please tell me you didn't go crazy on me and kill that bitch."

"No, Meeka, but I'm the reason she's out of prison. I sent the tape of Kindrah killing that doctor at my house that night, clearing Kelsey of the shooting."

"And why the fuck would you do some stupid shit like that? After all the shit that bitch put you through, you would risk her being back on the street to do it all over again?"

I sighed, not really in the mood to hear her go in on me. Even though I deserved it, I still wasn't feeling it.

"Your ass better be glad somebody offed the bitch," she said, laughing at my expense.

I didn't see anything funny about someone dying, and truth be told, if I had left her ass in prison, she wouldn't be dead right now.

In the back of my mind, I couldn't help but wonder if Amari had something to do with Kelsey being murdered.

"Hello? Lexi, you still on the line? Don't go getting quiet now that you fuck up. You sure you didn't kill that bitch?" she asked, laughing.

"No, Meeka, I didn't kill her. I need to go and let Amari know about Kelsey being killed," I said, ready to get off of the phone.

"Okay, but don't be surprised if that man tells you he killed the bitch," she said, getting serious.

"Girl, bye. I will talk to you later," I said, not totally blowing off her comment.

AMARI

Lexi told me what she saw on the news, and I couldn't help but think that she had something to do with Kelsey being killed. When I had gotten back home the night before, she wasn't home. She walked in at about 4 a.m., took a bath, and went downstairs. When she came back up and got in the bed, I just held her tight, because when I walked in the house that night, I thought she had left me. I was sick to my stomach at the thought of her leaving, so when she came home, I was so happy to see her.

Now she was telling me someone killed Kelsey. I wanted to ask her if she had anything to do with it, but I didn't. To be honest, I felt nothing of the news of Kelsey being killed. In fact, I was kind of relieved.

Lexi and I were sitting in the living room when the doorbell rang. It was two detectives at the door. I looked back at Lexi, who looked nervous. I'm not going to lie; I was nervous too.

"Mr. James, this is Detective Luke, and I'm Detective Jones. We are here with a few questions regarding the death of Ms. Kelsey Reed."

"I'm confused. What does Kelsey's death have to do with me?" I asked.

"Mr. James, can we please step inside? The quicker you answer the questions, the sooner we can be out of here."

Against my better judgment, I let them enter our home. Lexi sat on the couch, still looking guilty of something. I offered the detectives a seat and sat across from them, next to Lexi.

"Mr. James, we have reason to believe that Kelsey believed you to be the father of the baby she was carrying. Were you aware of this?"

I thought about lying, but thought better of it. Chances were that if they were asking, they already knew the answer.

"I just found out that she was claiming that I was the father of her unborn child and she wanted me to take a paternity test. She had papers sent to my home," I said, feeling like I was on trial.

"So, Mr. James, is there a possibility that you could have been the father of her child?"

"No. Kelsey and I were only friends, and I never had any sexual encounters with her," I said.

He stopped his line of questioning and began writing in his notepad, while his partner, Jones, picked up the line of questioning.

"Mrs. James, is it true that you contacted the district attorney with evidence that cleared Ms. Reed of murder charges?" he asked Lexi.

"Yes, but what does that have to do with her getting killed?" she stuttered.

My palms began to sweat. I just knew that they would be putting one of us in cuffs. Lexi had this mixture of guilt and fear on her face as the detective continued.

"Ms. Reed put your family through a lot. Why did you feel the need to clear her of all charges?" he asked.

"I just didn't feel right about her being behind bars for something she didn't do. Is that a crime?"

"No, it's not a crime; it's just strange. How do you feel about all the charges in your father-in-law's case being dismissed as well?"

"Well, I wasn't aware that she was cleared of those charges. That is news to myself and my husband," she said.

What the fuck did they mean she was cleared of all charges against my father too? I swear I could have killed that bitch.

"Well, we have all we need for right now. We will be conducting a thorough investigation, and I will be honest. Mr. James, right now, you and your wife have motive, meaning reason, to want to kill or have Ms. Reed killed. So right now, the both of you are suspects, and we ask that you don't leave town."

"Are you fucking serious? What motive do we have?" I asked, even though I knew the answer already.

"Mr. James, Ms. Reed sent you papers claiming you to be the father of her unborn child. Now, if she turns up dead, no test is needed. Correct? And your wife gets her released from prison, and now that she's out, once again causing problems for your family, what better way to stop her from doing it again? Death. Correct? So, like I said, don't leave town."

After the detectives left, Lexi and I looked at each other with questions in our eyes. Neither of us spoke, though, fearing the answers. We decided to go and pick up our children. I needed to see my babies.

It had taken Destiny and Miracle some time to get used to us. They cried for Kindrah, and it really broke our hearts, but Lexi, being the woman she was, gave them so much motherly love that they had no choice but to fall in love with her. I followed suit and did what came naturally, and they loved me now too. Tiara and Tiana loved their baby sisters. Our home had become a scene out of a daycare center, but I wouldn't trade it for anything in the world. I loved my kids and my stepdaughter, Imani.

The next few weeks were nerve-wracking as the detectives investigated the case. I will say that Lexi and I had a long talk about being honest with one another and never being scared to tell one another anything. I told her that I didn't kill Kelsey, and she insisted that she hadn't killed her either. I believed her.

We were having dinner one Friday evening when the doorbell rang, and I'm not going to lie, I was scared to death when I saw the detectives at the door. I didn't really want them in my home with the children there, but I invited them inside, hoping that they weren't coming to arrest me or Lexi. Lexi made sure the children were situated before she joined us in the living room.

"Mr. James, I want to apologize to you and your wife for all that we put you through, but understand that we were doing our job. We personally came by to inform you that you and your wife are no longer suspects in the murder of Kelsey Reed. In fact, we have Ms. Reed's killer in custody. Ms. Reed put her mother's boyfriend in jail over ten years ago, claiming he raped her. He was released from prison, still claiming his innocence, with revenge in mind. He set out to make her pay, and he succeeded by murdering her. He confessed, so again, I do apologize to you and your wife. Enjoy the rest of your evening."

Oh my God! I couldn't begin to explain what Lexi and I were feeling at that moment. I picked my wife up and hugged her, not wanting to let go. Imani, Tiana, and Tiara came running into the living room, joining in by hugging our legs. Lexi picked up Tiara, and I grabbed the other two, and we placed kisses all over their faces. I loved my family, and at the end of the day, that was all that mattered.